Praise for

The Man Who Fell to Earth

"Mesmerizing."   —*Philadelphia Inquirer*

"Entertainment of a high order. . . . Tevis makes you care
about his quirky characters. . . . [He] wrote like a dream,
and he told some wonderful stories."

—*Los Angeles Times*

"There is a rocking, hypnotic peacefulness in the way he
puts words together."   —*The Daily Beast*

"[Tevis is] a master manipulator of archetypes, an artist
capable of delving into the zeitgeist while nevertheless
remaining on his own pure search for himself."

—Jonathan Lethem

"Tevis has a gift for vivid characterization and propulsive
narrative. . . . His style is direct and efficient, never calling attention to itself; yet it grows in power through the
course of a novel by its very naturalness."

—Tobias Wolff

"[Tevis's] work is unique, with that element of infinite
rereadability Nabokov held the hallmark of great literature. Like his characters . . . Tevis's work will endure."

—*Fantasy & Science Fiction*

Walter Tevis

THE MAN WHO FELL TO EARTH

Walter Tevis is the author of *The Hustler*, *The Man Who Fell to Earth*, *Mockingbird*, *The Steps of the Sun*, *The Queen's Gambit*, *The Color of Money*, and the short story collection *Far from Home*. *The Man Who Fell to Earth* was the basis for a major motion picture starring David Bowie. *The Hustler* and *The Color of Money* were also adapted for film, *The Queen's Gambit* was the basis of the Emmy Award–winning Netflix series and *The Man Who Fell to Earth* is the basis of the Showtime series. Tevis died in 1984.

Also by Walter Tevis

The Hustler

Mockingbird

The Steps of the Sun

The Queen's Gambit

The Color of Money

Far from Home

THE MAN WHO FELL TO EARTH

THE MAN WHO FELL TO EARTH

Walter Tevis

Vintage Books
A Division of Penguin Random House LLC
New York

FIRST VINTAGE BOOKS EDITION 2022

Copyright © 1963 by Walter S. Tevis

All rights reserved. Published in the United States
by Vintage Books, a division of Penguin Random House LLC,
New York. Published in paperback in the United States
by Fawcett Gold Medal Books in 1963.

Vintage and colophon are registered
trademarks of Penguin Random House LLC.

The Cataloging-in-Publication Data is on file
at the Library of Congress.

Vintage Books Trade Paperback ISBN: 978-0-593-46747-3

Book design by Nicholas Alguire

www.vintagebooks.com

Printed in the United States of America
10 9 8 7 6 5 4 3 2 1

For Jamie
who knows Anthea better than I

And so it was I entered the broken world
To trace the visionary company of love, its voice
An instant in the wind (I know not whither hurled),
But not for long to hold each desperate choice.

HART CRANE

1985: ICARUS DESCENDING

CHAPTER ONE

AFTER TWO MILES of walking he came to a town. At the town's edge was a sign that read HANEYVILLE: POP. 1400. That was good, a good size. It was still early in the morning—he had chosen morning for the two-mile walk, because it was cooler then—and there was no one yet in the streets. He walked for several blocks in the weak light, confused at the strangeness—tense and somewhat frightened. He tried not to think of what he was going to do. He had thought about it enough already.

In the small business district he found what he wanted, a tiny store called The Jewel Box. On the street corner nearby was a green wooden bench, and he went to it and seated himself, his body aching from the labor of the long walk.

It was a few minutes later that he saw a human being.

It was a woman, a tired-looking woman in a shapeless blue dress, shuffling toward him up the street. He quickly averted his eyes, dumbfounded. She did not look right. He had expected them to be about his size, but this one was more than a head shorter than he. Her complexion was ruddier than he had expected, and darker. And the look, the *feel*, was strange— even though he had known that seeing them would not be the same as watching them on television.

Eventually there were more people on the street, and they were all, roughly, like the first one. He heard a man remark, in passing, "...like I say, they don't make cars like that one no more," and, although the enunciation was odd, less crisp than he had expected, he could understand the man easily.

Several people stared at him, a few of them suspiciously; but this did not worry him. He did not expect to be molested, and he was confident after observing the others that his clothes would bear up under inspection.

When the jewelry store opened he waited for ten minutes and then walked in. There was one man behind the counter, a small, chubby man in a white shirt and tie, dusting the shelves. The man stopped dusting, looked at him for a moment, a trifle strangely, and said, "Yes sir?"

He felt over tall, awkward. And suddenly very frightened. He opened his mouth to speak. Nothing came out. He tried to smile, and his face seemed to freeze. He felt, deep in him, something beginning to panic, and for a moment he thought he might faint.

The man was still staring at him, and his look seemed not to have changed. "Yes sir?" he said again.

By a great effort of will he was able to speak. "I ... I wonder if you might be interested in this ... ring?" How many times had he planned that innocuous question, said it over and over to himself? And yet now it rang strangely in his ears, like a ridiculous group of nonsense syllables.

The other man was still staring at him. "What ring?" he said.

"Oh." Somehow he managed a smile. He slipped the gold ring from the finger of his left hand and set it on the counter, afraid to touch the man's hand. "I . . . was driving through and my car broke down. A few miles down the road. I don't have any money; I thought perhaps I could sell my ring. It's quite valuable."

The man was turning the ring over in his hands, looking at it suspiciously. Finally he said, "Where'd you get this?"

The way the man said it made his breath choke in his throat. Could there be something wrong? The color of the gold? Something about the diamond? He tried to smile again. "My wife gave it to me. Several years ago."

The man's face was still clouded. "How do I know it isn't stolen?"

"Oh." The relief was exquisite. "My name is in the ring." He pulled his billfold from his breast pocket. "And I have identification." He took the passport out and set it on the counter.

The man looked at the ring and read aloud, "T. J. from Marie Newton, Anniversary, 1982," and then "18 K." He set the ring down, picked up the passport, and leafed through it. "England?"

"Yes, I'm an interpreter at the United Nations. This is my first trip here. Trying to see the country."

"Mmm," the man said, looking at the passport again. "I figured you talked with an accent." When he found the picture he read the name, "Thomas Jerome Newton," and then, looking up again, "No question about that. This is you, all right."

He smiled again, and this time the smile was more relaxed, more genuine, although he still felt lightheaded, strange—always there was the tremendous weight of his own body, the weight produced by the leaden gravity of this place. But he managed to say pleasantly, "Well then, would you be interested in buying the ring ...?"

He got sixty dollars for it, and knew that he had been cheated. But what he had now was worth more to him than the ring, more than the hundreds of rings just like it that he had with him. Now he had the first beginnings of confidence, and he had money.

With some of the money he bought a half-pound of bacon, six eggs, bread, a few potatoes, some vegetables—ten pounds of food altogether, all that he could carry. His presence aroused some curiosity, but no one asked questions, and he did not volunteer answers. It would not make any difference; he would not be back in that Kentucky town again.

When he left the town he felt well enough, in spite of all of the weight and the pain in his joints and in his back, for he had mastered the first step, he had made his start, he now owned his first American money. But when he was a mile from the town, walking through a barren field, toward the low hills where his camp was, all of it suddenly came over him in one crushing shock—the strangeness of it, the danger, the pain and worry in his body—and he fell to the ground and lay there, his body and his mind crying out against the violence that was being done to them by this most foreign, most strange and alien of all places.

He was sick: sick from the long, dangerous trip he had taken, sick from all the medicine—the pills, the inoculations, the inhaled gases—sick from worry, the anticipation of crisis, and terribly sick from the awful burden of his own weight. He had known for years that when the time came, when he would finally land and begin to effect that complex, long-prepared plan, he would feel something like this. This place, however much he had studied it, however much he had rehearsed his part in it, was so incredibly alien, the feeling—now that he *could* feel—the feeling was overpowering. He lay down in the grass and became very sick.

He was not a man; yet he was very much like a man. He was six and a half feet tall, and some men are even taller than that; his hair was as white as that of an albino, yet his face was a light tan color; and his eyes a pale blue. His frame was improbably slight, his features delicate, his fingers long, thin, and the skin almost translucent, hairless. There was an elfin quality to his face, a fine boyish look to the wide, intelligent eyes, and the white, curly hair now grew a little over his ears. He seemed quite young.

There were other differences, too: his fingernails, for example, were artificial, for he had none by nature. There were only four toes on each of his feet; he had no vermiform appendix and no wisdom teeth. It would have been impossible for him to develop hiccups, for his diaphragm, together with the rest of his breathing apparatus, was extremely sturdy, very highly developed. His chest expansion would have been about five inches. He weighed very little, about ninety pounds.

Yet he did have eyelashes, eyebrows, opposed thumbs, binocular vision, and a thousand of the physiological features of a normal human. He was incapable of warts; but stomach ulcers, measles and dental caries could affect him. He was human; but not, properly, a *man*. Also, man-like, he was susceptible to love, to fear, to intense physical pain and to self-pity.

After a half-hour he felt better. His stomach was still trembling and he felt as if he could not lift his head; but there was a sense that the first crisis was past and he began to look more objectively at the world around him. He sat up and looked across the field he was in. It was a grubby, flat pasture, with small areas of brown grass, of broom sage, and patches of glassy, re-frozen snow. The air was quite clear and the sky overcast, so that the light was diffused and soft and did not hurt his eyes as the glaring sunlight had two days before. There were a small house and a barn on the other side of the clump of dark and barren trees that fringed a pond. He could see the water of the pond through the trees, and the sight of it made his breath catch, for there was so much of it. He had seen it before like that, in his two days on Earth; but he was not yet used to it. It was another of those things that he had expected but was still a shock to see. He knew, of course, about the great oceans and about the lakes and rivers, had known about them since he was a boy; but the actual sight of the profusion of water in a single pond was breath-taking.

He began to see a kind of beauty in the strangeness of the field, too. It was quite different from what he had been taught to expect—as, he had already discovered, were many of the things of this world—yet there was pleasure now for him in its alien colors and textures, its new sights and smells. Its sounds, too; for his ears were very acute and he heard many strange and pleasant noises in the grass, the diverse rubbings and clickings of those insects that had survived the cold weather of early November; and even, with his head now against the ground, the very small, subtle murmurings in the earth itself.

Suddenly there was a fluttering in the air, an uprush of black wings, then hoarse, mournful calling, and a dozen crows flew overhead and away across the field. The Anthean watched them until they were out of sight, and then he smiled. This would be, after all, a fine world . . .

His camp was in a barren spot, carefully chosen—an abandoned eastern Kentucky coalfield. There was nothing within several miles of it but stripped ground, small patches of pale broom grass, and some outcroppings of sooty rock. Near one of these outcroppings his tent was pitched, barely visible against the rock. The tent was gray, and was made of what seemed to be cotton twill.

He was almost exhausted when he got there, and had to rest for several minutes before opening the sack and taking out the food. He did this carefully, putting on thin gloves before touching the packages, and then laying them on a small folding table. From beneath the table he withdrew a group of instruments, and set them beside the things he had bought in Haneyville. He looked for a moment at the eggs, potatoes, celery, radishes, rice, beans, sausage and carrots. He smiled for an instant, to himself. The food seemed innocent.

Then he picked up one of the small metallic devices, inserted an end of it into the potato, and began the qualitative analysis . . .

Three hours later he ate the carrot, raw, and took a bite out of the radish, which burned his tongue. The food was good—extremely strange, but good. Then he made a fire and boiled the egg and the potato. The sausage he buried—having found some amino-acids in it that he was not certain of. But there was no danger for him, except for the ever-present bacteria, in the other food. It was as they had hoped. He found the potato delicious, in spite of all the carbohydrates.

He was very tired. But before he lay down on his cot he went outside to look at the spot where he had destroyed the engine and instruments of his one-passenger craft two days before, his first day on Earth.

CHAPTER TWO

THE MUSIC WAS the Mozart *Clarinet Quintet in A Major*. Just before the final *allegretto*, Farnsworth adjusted the bass response on each of the pre-amplifiers and boosted the volume slightly. Then he settled himself ponderously in the leather armchair. He liked the *allegretto* with strong bass overtones; they gave the clarinet a resonance which, in itself, seemed to hold some kind of meaning. He stared at the curtain window that overlooked Fifth Avenue; he folded his plump fingers together, and listened to the music build.

When it had finished and the tape had cut off its own power, he looked over toward the doorway that led into the outer office and saw that the maid was standing there patiently, waiting for him. He glanced at the porcelain clock on the mantel and frowned. Then he looked at the maid and said, "Yes?"

"A Mr. Newton is here, sir."

"Newton?" He knew no wealthy Newtons. "What does he want?"

"He didn't say, sir." Then she raised one eyebrow slightly. "He's odd, sir. And he looks very . . . important."

He thought for a moment, and then said, "Show him in."

The maid had been right: the man was very odd. Tall, thin, with white hair and a fine, delicate bone structure. He had smooth skin and a boyish face—but the eyes were very strange, as though they were weak, over-sensitive, yet with a look that was old and wise and tired. The man wore an expensive dark gray suit. He walked to a chair and sat down carefully— easing himself into the seat as if he were carrying a great deal of weight. Then he looked at Farnsworth and smiled. "Oliver Farnsworth?"

"Would you like a drink, Mr. Newton?"

"A glass of water, please."

Farnsworth mentally shrugged his shoulders and relayed the order to the maid. Then, when she had left, he looked at his guest and leaned slightly forward with that universal gesture which means, "Let's get on with it."

Newton, however, remained sitting erect, his long, thin hands folded in his lap, and said, "You are good with patents, I understand?" There was a trace of an accent in his voice and his enunciation was too precise, too formal. Farnsworth could not identify the accent.

"Yes," Farnsworth said, and then somewhat curtly, "I have office hours, Mr. Newton."

Newton seemed not to hear this. His tone was gentle, warm. "I understand, in fact, that you are the best man in the United States with patents. Also that you are very expensive."

"Yes. I'm good."

"Fine," the other said. He reached down beside his chair and lifted his brief-case.

"And what do you want?" Farnsworth looked at the clock again.

"I would like to plan some things with you." The tall man was taking an envelope from his case.

"Isn't it pretty late?"

Newton had opened the envelope and he now withdrew a thin sheaf of bills, wrapped with a rubber band. He looked up and smiled genially. "Would you please come and get these? It is very difficult for me to walk. My legs."

Annoyed, Farnsworth pulled himself up from his chair, walked to the tall man, took the money, returned, and sat down. They were thousand-dollar bills.

"There are ten of them," Newton said.

"You're being pretty damn melodramatic, aren't you?" He put the stack into the pocket of his lounging-jacket. "Now what's this for?"

"For tonight," Newton said. "For about three hours of your close attention."

"But why, for heaven's sake, at night?"

The other shrugged his shoulders casually. "Oh, several reasons. Privacy is one of them."

"You could have had my attention for less than ten thousand dollars."

"Yes. But I also wanted to impress you with the . . . importance of our talk."

"Well." Farnsworth settled back in his chair, "Let's talk."

The thin man seemed relaxed, but he did not lean back. "First," he said, "how much money do you make a year, Mr. Farnsworth?"

"I'm not on salary."

"Well then. How much money did you make *last* year?"

"All right. You've paid for it. About one hundred forty thousand."

"I see. You are, as these things go, then, wealthy?"

"Yes."

"But you'd like more?"

This was becoming ridiculous. It was like a cheap television program. But the other man was paying; it was best to go along with it. He took a cigarette from a leather case and said, "Of course I'd like more."

Newton leaned just a bit forward this time. "A great deal more, Mr. Farnsworth?" he said, smiling, beginning to enjoy the situation enormously.

This was television too, of course, but it got across. "Yes," he said, and then, "Cigarette?" He held the case out to his guest.

Ignoring the offer, the man with the white, curly hair said, "I can make you very rich, Mr. Farnsworth, if you can devote your next five years entirely to me."

Farnsworth kept his face expressionless, lit his cigarette while his mind worked rapidly, turning this whole strange interview over, puzzling with the situation, with the slim possibility of this man's offer being sane. But the man, freak that he might be, had money. It would be wise to play along for a while. The maid came in with a silver tray with glasses and ice.

Newton took his glass of water from the tray gingerly, and then held it with one hand while he withdrew an aspirin box from his pocket with the other, flipped it open with his thumb, and dropped one of the pills into the water. The pill dissolved, white and murky. He held the glass and watched it for a moment, and then began sipping, extremely slowly.

Farnsworth was a lawyer; he had an eye for detail. He saw instantly that there was something odd about the aspirin box.

It was a common object, obviously a box of Bayer aspirin; but there was something about it that was wrong. And something was not right about the way that Newton was sipping the water, slowly, careful not to spill a drop—as if it were precious. And the water had clouded from one aspirin; that seemed wrong. He would have to try it with an aspirin later, when the man was gone, and see what happened.

Before the maid left, Newton asked her to take his brief-case to Farnsworth. When she had gone he took a last, loving sip and set his glass, still nearly full, beside him on the table. "There are some things in the brief-case I'd like you to read."

Farnsworth opened the bag, found a thick sheaf of papers and pulled them out on to his lap. The paper, he noticed immediately, had an unusual feel. Extremely thin, it was hard and yet flexible. The top sheet consisted mostly of chemical formulae neatly printed in bluish ink. He shuffled through the rest: circuit diagrams, charts, and schematic drawings of what appeared to be plant equipment. Tools and dies. At a glance, some of the formulae seemed familiar. He looked up. "Electronics?"

"Yes. Partly. You are familiar with that kind of equipment?"

Farnsworth did not answer. If the other man knew anything about him at all, he knew that he had fought half a dozen battles, as leader of a group of nearly forty lawyers, for the corporate life of one of the largest electronics parts manufacturing combines in the world. He began reading the papers . . .

Newton sat erect in his chair, looking at him, his white hair gleaming in the light from the chandelier. He was smiling; but his entire body ached. After a while he picked up his glass and began to sip the water that for all of his long life had been the most precious of all things at his home. He sipped slowly and watched Farnsworth read, and the tension he had felt, the carefully concealed anxiety that this utterly strange office in this still strange world had given him, the fright that this fat human, with his bulging jowls, his taut-skinned head and his little, porcine eyes, had made him feel, began to leave him. He knew now that he had this man; he had come to the right place . . .

More than two hours passed before Farnsworth looked up from the papers. During that time he drank three glasses of whisky. His eyes were pink at the corners. He blinked at Newton, at first hardly seeing him and then focusing on him, his small eyes wide.

"Well?" Newton said, still smiling.

The fat man took a breath, then shook his head as if trying to clear his mind. When he spoke, his voice was soft, hesitant, extremely cautious. "I don't understand them all," he said. "Only a few. A few. I don't understand optics—or photographic films." He looked back to the papers in his hand, as if making sure they were still there. "I'm a lawyer, Mr. Newton," he said. "I'm a lawyer." And then, suddenly, his voice came alive, trembling and strong, his fat body and his tiny eyes intent, alert. "But I know electronics. And I know dyes. I think I understand your . . . amplifier and I think I understand your television, and . . ." He paused for a moment, blinking, "My God, I think they can be manufactured the way you say they can." He let out his breath, slowly. "They look convincing, Mr. Newton. I think they will work."

Newton was still smiling at him. "They will work. All of them."

Farnsworth took out a cigarette and lit it, calming himself. "I'll have to check them. The metals, the circuits . . ." And then, suddenly, interrupting himself, the cigarette clutched between his fat fingers, "Good God, man, do you know what all of this means? Do you know that you have nine basic—that's *basic*—patents here?" He raised one paper in a pudgy hand, "Here in just the video transmission and in that little rectifier? And . . . do you know what that means?"

Newton's expression did not change. "Yes. I know what it means," he said.

Farnsworth inhaled slowly from his cigarette. "If you're right, Mr. Newton," he said, his voice becoming calmer now, "if you're right you can have RCA, Eastman Kodak. My Lord, you can have DuPont. Do you know what you have here?"

Newton stared hard at him. "I know what I have here," he said.

It took them six hours to drive to Farnsworth's country home. Newton tried to keep up their conversation for part of the time, bracing himself in the corner of the limousine's backseat, but the heavy accelerations of the car were too blindingly painful to his body, already overloaded with the pull of a gravitation that he knew it would take him years to become used to, and he was forced to tell the lawyer that he was very tired and needed to rest. Then he closed his eyes, let the cushioned back of the seat bear his weight as much as possible, and withstood the pain as well as he could. The air in the car was very warm to him, too—the temperature of their hottest days at home.

Eventually, as they passed beyond the edge of the city, the chauffeur's driving became more steady, and the painful jerks of stopping and starting began to subside. He glanced a few times at Farnsworth. The lawyer was not dozing. He was sitting with his elbows on his knees, still shuffling through the papers that Newton had given him, his little eyes bright, intense.

The house was an immense place, isolated in a great wooded area. The building and the trees seemed wet, glistening dimly in the gray morning light that was much like the light of midday of Anthea. It was refreshing to his over-sensitive eyes. He liked the woods, the quiet sense of life in them, and the glistening moisture—the sense of water and of fruitfulness that this earth overflowed with, even down to the continual trilling and chirping sounds of the insects. It would be an endless source of delight compared to his own world, with the dryness, the emptiness, the soundlessness of the broad, empty deserts between the almost deserted cities where the only sound was the whining of the cold and endless wind that voiced the agony of his own, dying people . . .

A servant, sleepy-eyed and wearing a bathrobe, met them at the door. Farnsworth dismissed the man with an order for coffee, and then shouted after him that he must have a room prepared for his guest and that he would receive no telephone calls for at least three days. Then Farnsworth led him into the library.

The room was very big and even more expensively decorated than the study in the New York apartment had been. Obviously Farnsworth read the best rich men's magazines. In the center of the floor was a white statue of a naked woman holding an elaborate lyre. Two of the walls were covered with bookshelves, and on the third was a large painting of a religious figure whom Newton recognized as Jesus, nailed to a wooden cross. The face in the picture startled him for a moment—with its thinness and large piercing eyes it could have been the face of an Anthean.

Then he looked at Farnsworth, who, although bleary-eyed, was more composed now, leaning back in his armchair, his small hands clasped together over his belly, looking at his guest. Their eyes met for an embarrassed moment, and the lawyer turned his away.

Then, in a moment, he looked back and said, quietly, "Well, Mr. Newton, what are your plans?"

He smiled. "They're very simple. I want to make as much money as possible. As quickly as possible."

There was no expression on the lawyer's face, but his voice was wry. "Your simplicity has elegance, Mr. Newton," he said. "How much money did you have in mind?"

Newton gazed distractedly at the expensive *objets d'art* in the room. "How much can we make in, say, five years?"

Farnsworth looked at him a moment, and then stood up. He waddled tiredly over to the bookshelf and began turning some small knobs there until speakers, hidden somewhere in the room, began playing violin music. Newton did not recognize the melody; but it was quiet and complex. Then, adjusting the dials, Farnsworth said, "That depends on two things."

"Yes?"

"First, how fairly do you want to play, Mr. Newton?"

Newton refocused his attention on Farnsworth. "Completely fairly," he said. "Legally."

"I see." Farnsworth could not seem to get the treble control adjusted to suit him. "Well then, second: what will my share be?"

"Ten percent of the net profits. Five percent of all corporate holdings."

Abruptly, Farnsworth took his fingers off the amplifier controls. He returned slowly to his chair. Then he smiled faintly. "All right, Mr. Newton," he said. "I think I can give you a net worth of . . . three hundred million dollars, within five years."

Newton thought for a moment about this. Then he said, "That won't be enough."

Farnsworth stared at him for a long minute, his eyebrows high, before he said, "Not enough for *what*, Mr. Newton?"

Newton's eyes hardened. "For a . . . research project. A very expensive one."

"I'll warrant it is."

"Suppose," the tall man said, "that I could provide you with a petroleum refining process about fifteen percent more efficient than any now in use? Would that bring your figure up to five hundred million?"

"Could your . . . process be set up within a year?"

Newton nodded. "Within a year it could be out-producing the Standard Oil Company—to whom, I suppose, we might lease it."

Farnsworth was staring again. Finally he said, "We'll start drawing up the papers tomorrow."

"Good." Newton rose stiffly from his chair. "We can talk about the arrangements in more detail then. There are, really, only two important considerations: that you get the money honestly, and that I be required to have little contact with anyone but you."

His bedroom was upstairs, and for a moment he thought he would not be able to climb the stairway. But he made it, a step at a time, while Farnsworth climbed beside him, saying nothing. Then, after he had shown him to his room, the lawyer looked at him and said, "You're an unusual man, Mr. Newton. Do you mind if I ask where you are from?"

The question came as a complete surprise, but he kept his composure. "Not at all," he said, "I'm from Kentucky, Mr. Farnsworth."

The lawyer's eyebrows rose only slightly. "I see," he said. Then he turned and walked ponderously away down the hall, which was floored with marble and caused his footsteps to echo . . .

His room was high-ceilinged and ornately furnished. He noticed a television set built into the wall in such a way that it could be viewed from the bed and he smiled tiredly on seeing it—he would have to watch it sometime, to see how their reception compared with that on Anthea. And it would be amusing to see some of the shows again. He had always liked the Westerns, even though the quiz programs and the Sunday "educational" shows had provided his staff at home with most of the information that he had memorized. He had not seen a television show in . . . how long had the trip taken? . . . four months. And he had been on Earth two months—getting money, studying the disease germs, studying the food and water, perfecting his accent, reading the newspapers, preparing himself for the critical interview with Farnsworth.

He looked out the window at the brighter light of morning, at the pale blue sky. Somewhere in the sky, possibly directly where he was looking, was Anthea. A cold place, dying, but one for which he could be homesick; a place where there were people whom he loved, people whom he would not see again for a very long time . . . But he would see them again.

He closed the curtains at the window, and then, gently, eased his tired, aching body into bed. Somehow all of the excitement seemed gone, and he was placid and calm. He fell asleep within a few minutes.

Afternoon sunlight woke him, and even though it hurt his eyes with its brilliance—for the curtains at the window were translucent—he awoke feeling rested and pleasant. Possibly it was the softness of the bed compared with those in the obscure hotels where he had been staying, and possibly it was relief at the success of last night. He lay in bed, thinking, for several minutes and then got up and went into the bathroom. There was an electric razor laid out for him, together with soap, washcloth and towel. He smiled at this, Antheans did not have beards. He turned the lavatory tap on and watched it for a moment, fascinated as ever with the sight of all that water. Then he washed his face, not using the soap—for it was irritating to his skin—but using a cream from a jar in his brief-case. Then he took his usual pills, changed his clothes, and went downstairs to begin earning a half billion dollars . . .

That evening, after six hours of talking and planning, he stood for a long time on the balcony outside his room, enjoying the cool air and looking at the black sky. The stars and the planets seemed strange, shimmering in the heavy atmosphere, and he enjoyed staring at them, in their unfamiliar positions. But he knew little of astronomy, and the patterns were confusing to him—except for those of the Big Dipper and a few minor constellations. Finally he returned to his room. It would have been pleasant to know which one was Anthea; but he could not tell . . .

CHAPTER THREE

ON AN UNSEASONABLY warm spring afternoon Professor Nathan Bryce, walking up the stairs to his fourth-floor apartment, discovered a roll of caps on the third-floor landing. Remembering the last afternoon's loud banging of cap guns in the hallways, he picked this up with the intention of flushing it down the toilet when he reached his apartment. It had taken him a moment to recognize the little roll, for it was bright yellow. When he was a boy, caps had always been red, a peculiar rust shade, and that had always seemed the right color for caps and firecrackers, and that kind of thing. But apparently they were making yellow ones now, as they made pink refrigerators and yellow aluminum drinking glasses, and other such incongruous wonders. He continued up the stairs, perspiring, thinking now of some of the chemical subtleties that went into even the making of yellow spun-aluminum drinking glasses. He speculated that the cave-men who drank from their cupped and calloused hands might have done perfectly well for themselves

without all the complex learning in chemical engineering—
that ungodly, sophisticated knowledge of molecular behavior
and of commercial processes—which he, Nathan Bryce, was
paid to know and to publish research papers about.

By the time he reached his apartment he had forgotten the
caps. There were too many other things to be thought of. Still
sitting where it had sat for the past six weeks, on one side of his
big, scarred oak desk, was a disordered pile of student papers,
horrible to contemplate. Next to the desk was an ancient, gray
painted steam radiator, an anachronism in these days of electrical heating, and on its venerable ironwork cover was stacked
a disorderly, menacing pile of student lab notebooks. These
were piled so high that the little Lasansky print that hung well
clear of the radiator was almost completely covered by them.
Only a pair of heavy-lidded eyes showed—the eyes, possibly,
of a weary god of science, peering in mute anguish over laboratory reports. Professor Bryce, being a man given to a peculiar
kind of wry whimsy, thought of this. He also noted the fact
that the little print—it was the bearded face of a man—one of
the few worthwhile things he had encountered in three years
in this Midwestern town, was now impossible to see because
of the work of his, Bryce's, students.

On the uncluttered side of his desk his typewriter sat like
another mundane god—a boorish, trivial, over-demanding
god—still holding the seventeenth page of a paper on the
effects of ionizing radiations upon polyester resins, a paper
unsought, unhonored and one that would probably always
remain unfinished. Bryce's gaze met this sullen disarray: the
scattered paper sheets like a fallen, bombed-out city of card
houses, the endless, frighteningly neat student solutions of

oxidation-reduction equations and of the industrial prepara-
tions of unlovely acids; the equally dull, dull paper on polyester
resins. He stared at these things, his hands in the pocket of
his coat, for a full thirty seconds, in blank dismay. Then, since
it was hot in the room, he pulled off his coat, threw it on the
gold brocade couch, reached under his shirt to scratch his belly,
and walked into the kitchen and began making coffee. The sink
was littered with dirty retorts, beakers and small jars, together
with the breakfast dishes, one of them smeared with egg yolk.
Looking at this impossible confusion he felt for a moment like
screaming with despair; but he did not. He merely stood for
a minute and then said, softly, aloud, "Bryce, you're a damn
mess." Then he found a reasonably clean beaker, rinsed it out,
filled it with powdered coffee and hot tap water, stirred it with
a lab thermometer, and drank it off, staring over the beaker
at the big, expensive Brueghel print of *The Fall of Icarus* that
hung on the wall above the white stove. A fine picture. It was
a picture that he had once loved but was now merely used to.
The pleasure it gave him now was only intellectual—he liked
the color, the forms, the things a dilettante likes—and he knew
perfectly well that was supposed to be a bad sign and further-
more that the feeling had much to do with the unhappy pile
of papers surrounding his desk in the next room. Finishing
the coffee, he quoted, in a soft, ritualistic voice, without any
particular expression or feeling, the lines from Auden's poem
about the painting:

> ". . . *the expensive delicate ship that must have seen*
> *Something amazing, a boy falling out of the sky,*
> *Had somewhere to get to and sailed calmly on."*

He set the beaker down, unrinsed, on the stove. Then he rolled up his sleeves, took off his tie, and began filling the sink with hot water, watching the detergent foam bubble up under the pressure from the faucet like a multicelled living thing, the compound eye of a huge albino insect. Then he began putting glassware through the foam, into the hot water beneath it. He found the dishwashing sponge and began working. He had to start somewhere . . .

Four hours later he had collected a small stack of graded term papers and began fumbling in his pocket for a rubber band to fasten them into a bundle. It was then he discovered the roll of caps. He pulled it from his pocket, held it in the palm of his hand for a moment, and then grinned foolishly. He hadn't shot a cap for thirty years—not since, at some time of ancient, pimply innocence, he had gone from cap guns and *A Child's Garden of Verses* to the giant, official-looking Chem-Craft set that had been given him by his grandfather as a direct prod from Fate. Suddenly he found himself wishing he had a cap gun; he felt that, here, in his empty apartment, he would like to shoot the caps off, one by one. And then he remembered how, once, God knew how many years ago, he had wondered what would happen if you set a whole roll of caps afire—a delightful, radical idea. But he had never tried it. Well, there was no better time. He got up, smiling wearily, and went into the kitchen. He set the roll of caps on a sheet of copper gauze, put the sheet on a tripod stand, poured a little alcohol from an alcohol lamp on them, muttering pedantically, "Positive ignition," took a wood splinter from a stack, lit it with his cigarette lighter, and then cautiously touched off the caps. He was surprised and pleased by the results; expecting only an irregular series of little *phrrt* sounds and some gray gunsmoke, he got instead, while the roll danced madly on the wire gauze, a fine confusion of loud, sat-isfying *bangs*. Strangely, no smoke rose from the black residue. He bent and sniffed the little black mass that was left. No odor at all. That was odd. My God, he thought, how fast things hap-pen! Some other poor fool of a chemist had found a substitute for gunpowder already. He wondered briefly what it could be and then shrugged. Maybe he'd look into it some time. But he missed the smell of gunpowder—a fine, pungent smell. He looked at his watch. Seven-thirty. Outside the windows was spring twilight. It was past supper-time. He went into the bathroom, washed his hands and face, shaking his head at his own gray haggardness in the mirror. Then he picked up his coat from the couch, put it on and went out. Vaguely, walking downstairs, he scanned the steps for another roll of caps, but there was none.

After a hamburger and a cup of coffee he decided to go to a movie. He'd had a hard day—four hours of lab work, three hours of teaching, four hours of reading those idiot papers. He walked downtown, hoping there would be a science fic-tion movie—one with resurrected dinosaurs clomping around Manhattan in bird-brained wonder, or insectivorous invaders from Mars, come to destroy the whole damn world (and good riddance, too), so they could eat the bugs. But nothing like that was playing, and he settled for a musical, buying popcorn and a candy bar before going in to the dark little auditorium and searching out an isolated seat on the aisle. He began eating the popcorn, trying to get the taste of the cheap mustard from the hamburger out of his mouth. A newsreel was in progress and he watched it dully, with the mild dread that such things could give him. There were pictures of riots in Africa. *How many years have they been rioting in Africa? Ever since the early sixties?*

There was a speech by a Gold Coast politician, threatening the use of "tactical hydrogen weapons" against some hapless "fomenters." Bryce squirmed in his seat, ashamed for his profession. Years before, as a graduate student of brilliant promise, he had worked for a while on the original H-bomb project. Like poor old Oppenheimer, he had had his serious doubts even then. The newsreel shifted to pictures of missile emplacements along the Congo River, then to the manned rocket races in Argentina, and finally to New York fashions, featuring off-the-bosom gowns for women, and men's frilly trousers. But Bryce could not get the Africans out of his mind; those serious young black men were the grandsons of the dusty, sullen family groups in the *National Geographics*, thumbed through in innumerable doctors' offices and in the parlors of respectable relatives. He remembered the sagging breasts of the women, the inevitable red scarf or scarlet handkerchief in every color photograph. Now the descendants of those people were wearing uniforms and going to universities, drinking martinis, making their own hydrogen bombs.

The musical came on in strong vulgar colors, as if, by glaring force, it could erase the memory of the newsreel. It was called *The Shari Leslie Story*, and was dull and noisy. Bryce tried to lose himself in the aimless movement and color, but found he could not and had to content himself at first with the tight bosoms and long legs of the young women in the picture. This was distracting enough in itself, but it was the kind of distraction that could be painful, as well as absurd, for a middle-aged widower. Squirming, confronted by blatant sensuality, he shifted his attention to the photography, and became for the first time aware that the technical quality of the images was striking. The line and detail, though blown up on a huge

Dupliscope screen, appeared as sharp as in a contact print. He blinked, seeing this now, and then cleaned his glasses on his handkerchief. There was no doubt of it, the images were perfect. He knew a smattering of photochemistry; this quality did not seem quite possible, with what he knew of dye-transfer processes and three-emulsion color films. He caught himself whistling softly in astonishment, and watched the rest of the movie with a greater interest—only occasionally distracted when one of the pink images would peel off a brassiere— a thing he had never got used to in the movies.

Afterward, on his way out of the theater, he stopped a moment to look at the advertisements for the film, to see what they might say about the color process. This was not at all hard to find; blazoned across the garish ads was a banner that read: IN THE NEW, NEW COLOR SENSATION WORLDCOLOR. There was, however, nothing more than this, except for the little circled R that meant "registered trade mark," and in infinitesimal print, below, Registered by W. E. Corp. He fished around in his mind for combinations that would fit the initials, but with the freakish whimsicality that his mind would sometimes produce, the only things he found were absurd: Wan Eagles, Wamsutta Enchiladas, Wealthy Engineers, Worldly Eros. He shrugged his shoulders, and, hands in his pants pockets, began walking down the evening street, into the neon heart of the little college town.

Restless, a little irritated, not wanting just yet to have to go home and stare at those papers again, he found himself looking for one of the beer parlors where the students hung out. He found one, a small taproom named Henry's, an arty little place with German beer mugs in the front windows. He had been there before, but only in the mornings. This was one of

his few active vices. He had found, since the time eight years
ago when his wife had died (in a glossy hospital, with a three-
pound tumor in her stomach), that there were certain things
to be said in favor of drinking in the mornings. He had discovered, quite by accident, that it could be a fine thing, on a
gray, dismal morning—a morning of limp, oyster-colored
weather—to be gently but firmly drunk, making a pleasure
of melancholy. But it had to be undertaken with a chemist's
precision; bad things could happen in the event of a mistake.
There were nameless cliffs that could be fallen over, and on
gray days there were always self-pity and grief nibbling about,
like earnest mice, at the corner of morning drunkenness. But
he was a wise man, and he knew about these matters. Like
morphine it all depended upon proper measurements.

He opened the door of Henry's and was greeted by the sub-
dued agony of a juke box that dominated the center of the room,
pulsating with bass sound and red light, like a diseased and frenetic heart. He walked in, a little unsteadily, between rows of
plastic booths, normally empty and colorless in the mornings,
now jammed with students. Some of them were muttering
earnestly; many were bearded and fashionably shabby—like
theatrical anarchists, or "agents of a foreign power" from the
old, old movies of the thirties. And behind the beards? Poets?
Revolutionaries? One of them, a student in his organic chemistry course, wrote articles for the student paper about free love
and the "decayed corpse of the Christian ethic, polluting the
well-springs of life." Bryce nodded to him, and the boy gave
him an embarrassed glare, over the sulky beard. Nebraska and
Iowa farm boys, most of them, signing disarmament petitions,
discussing socialism. For a moment he felt uneasy; a tired old
Bolshevik wearing a tweed coat amid the new class.

He found a narrow space at the bar and ordered a glass of beer from a woman with graying bangs and black-rimmed glasses. He had never seen her there before; he was served in the mornings by a taciturn and dyspeptic old man named Arthur. This woman's husband? He smiled at her vaguely, taking the beer. He gulped at it quickly, feeling uncomfortable, wanting to get out. On the juke box, now behind his head, a record had started playing a folk song, with a zither thrumming metallically. *Oh Lordie, Pick A Bale of Cotton! Oh Lordie* ... Next to him at the bar a white girl was talking to a sad-eyed black girl about the "structure" of poetry and asking her if the poem "worked," a kind of talk that made Bryce shudder. How goddamned knowing could these children be? Then he remembered the cant he had talked, during the year that he had majored in English, when he was in his twenties: "levels of meaning," "the semantic problem," "the symbolical level." Well, there were plenty of substitutes for knowledge and insight—false metaphors everywhere. He finished his beer and then, not knowing why, ordered another, even though he wanted to leave, to get away from the noise and the posturing. And wasn't he being unfair to these kids, being a pompous ass? Young people always looked foolish, were deceived by appearances—as was everybody else. Better they should grow beards than join fraternities or become debaters. They would learn enough about that kind of bland idiocy soon enough, when they got out of school, new-shaven, and looked for jobs. Or was he wrong there too? There was always the chance that they—at least some of them—were honest-to-God Ezra Pounds, would never shave the beards, would become brilliant and shrill Fascists, Anarchists, Socialists, and die in unheard-of European cities, the authors of fine poems, the painters of meaningful pictures, men of no fortune, and with a name to come. He finished the beer and had another. Drinking it, there flashed across his mind the image of the theater poster and the giant word, Worldcolor, and it occurred to him that the W of W. E. Corp. might stand for Worldcolor. Or, perhaps, World. And the E? *Elimination? Exhibitionism? Eroticism?* Or, he smiled grimly, just *Exit?* He smiled wisely at the red-jacketed girl next to him, who was talking now about the "texture" of language. She could not have been more than eighteen. She gave him a dubious look, her dark eyes serious. And then he felt something hurt him; she was so pretty. He stopped smiling, finished his beer quickly, and left. As he passed the booth on the way out, the Organic Chemistry student with the beard said, "Hello, Professor Bryce," his voice very decent. Bryce nodded to him, mumbled, and pushed his way out the door into the warm night.

It was eleven o'clock, but he did not want to go home. For a moment he thought of calling Gelber, his one close friend on the Faculty, but decided not to. Gelber was a sympathetic man; but there did not seem to be anything to say right now. He did not want to talk about himself, his fear, his cheap lust, his dreadful and foolish life. He kept walking.

Just before midnight he stopped in the town's one all-night drugstore, empty except for an aged clerk behind the gleaming, plastic lunch counter. He sat down and ordered coffee and, after his eyes became accustomed to the false brilliance of the fluorescent lights, began to gaze idly about the counter, reading the display labels on aspirin bottles, camera equipment, packages of razor blades . . . He was squinting, and his head was beginning to hurt. The beer; the light . . . Sun tan lotion and pocket combs. And then something caught his eyes and held them. Worldcolor: 35 mm Camera Film, printed on each of a row of square blue boxes, next to the pocket combs, under a card of nail clippers. It startled him, he did not know why. The clerk was standing near, and abruptly Bryce said, "Let me see that film, please."

The clerk squinted at him—did the light hurt his eyes too?—and said, "What film?"

"The color. Worldcolor."

"Oh. I didn't—"

"Sure, I know." He was surprised that his voice was impatient. He wasn't in the habit of interrupting people.

The old man frowned slightly, and then shuffled over and pulled down a box of the film. Then he set it down on the counter in front of Bryce, with exaggerated firmness, saying nothing.

Bryce picked up the box and looked at the label. Under the big letters was printed, in small letters: A Grainless, Perfectly Balanced Color Film. And below this: ASA film speed: 200 to 3,000 depending upon development. *My God!* he thought, *The speed can't be that high. And variable?*

He looked up at the clerk. "How much is this?"

"Six dollars. That's for thirty-six pictures. For twenty it's two seventy-five."

He felt the box, which was light in his hand. "That's pretty expensive, isn't it?"

The clerk grimaced, in some kind of old man's annoyance. "Not when you don't pay for developing it."

"Oh, I see. They develop it for you. You get a mailing envelope . . ." He broke off. This was a stupid conversation. Somebody has invented a new film. What did he care? He wasn't a photographer.

After a pause, the clerk said, "No." And then, turning away, toward the door, "It develops itself."

"It what?"

"Develops itself. Look, you want to buy the film?"

Not answering, he turned the box over in his hand. On each end was printed, boldly, the words, SELF-DEVELOPING. And it struck him: why haven't I heard about this in the chemical journals? A new process . . .

"Yes," he said, distractedly, looking at the label. There, at the bottom, was the fine print: W. E. Corp. "Yes. I'll buy it." He fumbled his billfold out, and gave the man six crumpled bills. "How does it work?"

"You put it back in the can." The man picked up the money. He seemed soothed by it, less truculent.

"Back in the can?"

"The little can that it comes in. You put it back in the can when you've shot all your pictures. Then you press a little button on top of the can. It tells you. There's directions inside. You press the button once, or more times—depends on what they call 'film speed.' That's all there is to it."

"Oh." He stood up, his coffee unfinished, putting the box gingerly in his coat pocket. Leaving, he asked the clerk, "How long has this stuff been on the market?"

"The film? About two, three weeks. Works fine. We sell a lot of it."

He walked directly home, wondering about the film. How could anything be that good, that easy? Absently, he pulled the box from his pocket, peeled it open with his thumbnail. Inside was a blue metal can, with a screw top, a red button sticking up from it. He opened it. Wrapped in a sheet of directions was an ordinary-looking cassette of 35 millimeter film. Under the canister top, beneath the button, was a small grid. He felt this with his thumbnail. It seemed to be made of porcelain.

At home, he dug an ancient Argus camera out of a drawer. Then, before loading it, he pulled about a foot of the film out of the cartridge, exposing it, and then tore it off. It felt dull to the touch, without the usual slickness of a gelatinous emulsion. Then he loaded the rest in the camera and exposed it rapidly, taking random pictures of the walls, the radiator, the pile of papers on his desk, shooting at an 800 speed in the dim light. Then, finished, he developed the film in the can, pressing the button eight times and then opening it, smelling the can as he did so. A faint bluish gas with an acrid, unrecognizable smell came out. There was no liquid in the can. Gaseous development? He took the film out hastily, pulling the strip from the cartridge, and, holding it up to the light, found a set of perfect transparencies, in fine, lifelike color and detail. He whistled aloud and said, "Goddamn." Then he took the piece of blank film, and the transparency strip, and went into the kitchen with them. He began setting up the materials for a quick analysis, arranging rows of beakers, getting out the titration equipment. He found himself working feverishly, and did not take the time to wonder what was making him so frenetically curious about this thing. Something about it was nagging at him, but he ignored it—he was too busy . . .

Five hours later, at six o'clock in the morning, with a gray and bird-noisy sky outside the window, he fell back wearily into a kitchen chair, holding a small piece of the film. He had not tried everything with it; but he had tried enough to know that none of the conventional chemicals of photography, none of the silver salts, were in the film. He sat, red-eyed and staring, for several minutes. Then he got up, walked with great weariness to his bedroom and fell, half-exhausted, on the unmade bed. Before he fell asleep, still dressed, with birds shouting outside his window and the sun rising, he said aloud, his voice wry and gravelly, "It's got to be a whole new technology . . . somebody digging up a science in the Mayan ruins . . . or from some other planet . . ."

CHAPTER FOUR

PEOPLE MOVED UP and down the sidewalks in shifting, fast-paced crowds, dressed in spring clothes. Everywhere there seemed to be young women, high heels clicking (he could hear them, even from the car), many of them brilliantly dressed, their clothes preternaturally bright in the strong morning light. Enjoying the sight of the people and the colors—even though they hurt his still over-sensitive eyes—he told his driver to go slowly down Park Avenue. It was a lovely day, one of the first truly bright days of his second spring on Earth. He leaned back, smiling, against the specially-designed back cushions and the car moved downtown at a slow and steady speed. Arthur, the driver, was very good; he had been chosen for his smoothness, his ability to hold speed steadily, to avoid sudden changes in movement.

They turned over to Fifth Avenue at midtown, pulling up in front of Farnsworth's old office building, which now bore, at one side of the entranceway, a brass plaque that read, in discreet, raised letters: WORLD ENTERPRISES CORPORATION. Newton adjusted his dark glasses to a darker shade, to protect against the outside sunlight, and eased himself out of the limousine. He stood on the pavement, stretching, feeling the sun—mildly warm to the people around him, pleasantly hot to him—on his face.

Arthur put his head out the window and said, "Shall I wait, Mr. Newton?"

He stretched again, enjoying the sunlight, the air. He had not left his apartment for over a month. "No," he said. "I'll call you, Arthur. But I doubt I'll need you before evening; you may go to a movie if you'd like."

He walked in, through the main hallway, past the rows of elevators, and down to the special elevator at the end of the hall, where an attendant awaited him, standing stiffly, his uniform impeccable. Newton smiled to himself; he could imagine the flurry of commands that must have gone out the day before, after he had called and said he would be coming in the next morning. He hadn't been in the offices for three months. It was seldom that he ever left his apartment. The elevator boy gave him a rehearsed and nervous, "Good morning, Mr. Newton." He smiled at him and stepped in.

The elevator took him slowly and very smoothly up to the seventh floor, which had formerly housed Farnsworth's law offices. Farnsworth was waiting for him when he stepped out. The lawyer was dressed like a potentate in a gray silk suit, a brilliant red jewel flashing on a fat and perfectly manicured ring finger. "You're looking well, Mr. Newton," he said, taking his extended hand with gentle care. Farnsworth was observant; he would have noticed, quickly enough, the wince that Newton made if he were touched roughly in any way.

"Thank you, Oliver. I've been feeling especially well."

Farnsworth led him down a hallway, past offices and into a suite of rooms with the plaque, W. E. Corp. They walked by a battery of secretaries, who became respectfully silent at their approach, and into Farnsworth's office, with O. V. Farnsworth, President, in small brass letters on the door.

Inside, the office was furnished as before, with mixed rococo pieces dominated by the huge, grotesquely ornamented Caffieri desk. The room was, as always, filled with music—a violin piece this time. It was unpleasant to Newton's ears; but he said nothing.

A maid brought them tea, while they chatted for a few minutes—Newton had learned to like tea, although he had to drink it lukewarm—and then they began to talk about business: their status in the courts, the arranging and rearranging of directorships, holding companies, grants and licenses and royalties, the financing of new plants, the purchase of old ones, the markets, prices, and the fluctuation of public interest in the seventy-three consumer articles they made—television antennae, transistors, photographic film and radiation detectors—and the three hundred-odd patents they leased out, from the oil refining process to a harmless substitute for gunpowder that was used in children's toys. Newton was well aware of Farnsworth's amazement—even more than usual—with his own grasp of these things, and he told himself it would be wise if he made a few intentional blunders in his recollection of figures and details. Yet it was enjoyable, exciting—even though he knew the vain and cheap pride that gave the pleasure—in using his Anthean mind on these matters. It was as if one of these people—he always thought of them as "these people," much as he had grown to like and to admire them—should find himself dealing with a group of very alert and resourceful chimpanzees. He was fond of them and, with his fundamental human vanity, unable to resist the easy pleasure of exercising his mental superiority to their dumbfounded amazement. Yet, enjoyable as this might be, he had to remember that these people were more dangerous than chimpanzees—and it had been thousands of years since any of them had seen an Anthean undisguised.

They went on talking until the maid brought them lunch— sliced-chicken sandwiches and a bottle of Rhine wine for Farnsworth; oatmeal cookies and a glass of water for Newton. Oatmeal, he had found, was one of the most digestible foods for the peculiar qualities of his system, and he ate it frequently. They continued to talk for quite a while about the complex business of financing the various and widespread enterprises. Newton had come to enjoy this part of the game for its own sake. He had been forced to learn it from scratch—there were many things about this society and this planet that could not be learned from watching television—and he had found he had a natural bent for it, possibly an atavism tracing back to ancient ancestors in the old, strong days that had been the glory of primitive Anthean culture. That was during the time that this earth had been in its second ice age—the time of harsh capitalism and warfare, before the Anthean power sources had been all but exhausted and the water gone. He enjoyed playing with the counters and the numbers of finance, even though this power gave him little excitement and though he had entered the game with the stacked deck that only ten thousand years of Anthean electronics, chemistry and optics could have provided. But he never for a moment forgot what he had come to Earth for. It was always with him, unavoidable, like the dim ache that still lived in his strengthened, but always tired, muscles, like the impossible strangeness, however familiar it would become, of this huge and various planet.

He enjoyed Farnsworth. He enjoyed the few humans he knew. He was unacquainted with any women, for he feared them, for reasons he did not understand himself. He was sad, sometimes, that security made it too risky to know these people better. Farnsworth, hedonist that he was, was a shrewd man, a lusty player of the game of money; a man who required occasional watching; a possibly dangerous man, but one whose mind had many fine and subtle facets. He had not made his huge income—an income that Newton had trebled for him—solely on reputation.

When he had made it clear enough to Farnsworth what he wanted to have done, he leaned back in his chair for a moment, resting, and then said, "Oliver, now that the money is beginning to ... accumulate, there is a new thing I want to undertake. I spoke to you before of a research project ..."

Farnsworth did not seem surprised. But then he had probably been expecting something more important to be the subject of this visit. "Yes, Mr. Newton?"

He smiled gently. "It will be a different kind of undertaking, Oliver. And, I fear, an expensive one. I imagine you'll have some work to do in setting it up—the financial end of it anyway." He looked out the window for a moment, at the discreet row of gray Fifth Avenue shops, and at the trees. "It's to be nonprofit, and I think the best thing is to set up a research foundation."

"A research foundation?" The lawyer pursed his lips.

"Yes." He turned back to Farnsworth. "Yes, I think we'll incorporate in Kentucky, with about all the capital I can gather together. That'll be about forty million dollars, I think—if we can get the banks to help us."

Farnsworth's eyebrows shot up. "*Forty million?* You're not worth half that, Mr. Newton. In another six months maybe, but we've only begun . . ."

"Yes, I know. But I think I'm going to sell my rights in Worldcolor to Eastman Kodak, outright. You may, of course, keep your share, if you wish. Eastman will make intelligent use of it, I imagine. They're prepared to go rather high to get it—with a proviso that I don't market a competitive color film within the next five years."

Farnsworth was getting red in the face now. "Isn't that like selling a life interest in the US Treasury?"

"I suppose it is. But I need the capital; and you know yourself that there's an annoying danger of anti-trust action inherent in those patents. And Kodak has better access to the world markets than we have. Really, we'll be saving ourselves a great deal of trouble."

Farnsworth shook his head, somewhat placated. "If I had a copyright on the Bible I wouldn't sell it to Random House. But I suppose you know what you're doing. You always do."

CHAPTER FIVE

AT PENDLEY STATE University in Pendley, Iowa, Nathan Bryce dropped by the office of his department head. This was Professor Canutti and his position was called Departmental Co-ordinator-Adviser, which was much like the titles of most department heads these days, since the time of the great labeling shift that had turned every salesman into a Field Representative, every janitor into a Custodian. It had taken a little longer to reach the universities. But it had reached them, and nowadays there were no more secretaries, only Receptionists and Administrative Aides, no more bosses, only Co-ordinators.

Professor Canutti, crew-cut, pipe-smoking and rubbery complexioned, welcomed him with a twenty-dollar smile, waved him across the pigeon's-egg blue carpet to a lavender plastic chair and said, "Good to see you, Nate."

Bryce winced almost visibly at the "Nate," and, looking at his watch as though in a hurry, said, "Something I'm curious about, Professor Canutti." He was not in a hurry—except to get this interview over with; now that exams were ended he had nothing to do for a week.

Canutti smiled sympathetically, and Bryce momentarily cursed himself for coming to see this golf-playing idiot in the first place. But Canutti might know something of use to him; he was at least no fool as a chemist.

Bryce pulled a box from his pocket, and set it on Canutti's desk. "Have you seen this new film?" he said.

Canutti picked it up in his soft, uncalloused hand, and looked at it for a moment, puzzled. "Worldcolor? Yes, I've used it, Nate." He set it down, with a kind of finality. "It's a darn good film. Self-developing."

"Do you know how it works?"

Canutti drew speculatively on his pipe, which was unlit. "No, Nate. Can't say as I do. Like any other film, I guess. Only a little more . . . sophisticated." He smiled at his pleasantry.

"Not exactly." Bryce reached over and picked up the box, weighing it in his hand, and watching Canutti's bland face. "I ran some tests on it, and was pretty thoroughly startled. You know, the best color films have three separate emulsions, one for each primary. Well, this one has no emulsion at all."

Canutti raised his eyebrows. *You'd better look surprised, you idiot*, Bryce thought. Taking the pipe from his mouth Canutti said, "Sounds impossible. Where's the photosensitivity?"

"Apparently in the base. And it seems to be done with barium salts—only God would know how. Crystalline barium salts in a random dispersion. And," he drew a breath, "the developer is gaseous—in a little pod under the canister lid. I've tried to find what's in it and all I can be certain of is potassium nitrate, some peroxide and something that, so help me, acted like cobalt. And it's all mildly radio-active, which may explain something, although I'm not certain what."

Canutti gave him the long pause that his little lecture, in all politeness, required. Then he said, "Sounds wild, Nate. Where do they make it?"

"There's a factory in Kentucky. But they're incorporated in New York, as near as I can find out. No stock listed on the exchange."

Canutti, listening, adopted a serious expression; probably, Bryce thought, the one he reserved for solemn occasions, like being admitted to a new country club. "I see. Well, that is tricky, isn't it?"

Tricky? What in hell did that mean? Of course it was tricky. It was impossible. "Yes, it's tricky. That's what I wanted to ask you about." He hesitated a moment, reluctant to ask a favor of this pompous little extrovert. "I'd like to follow it up, find out how the devil it works. I wonder if I could use one of the big research labs down in the basement—at least during the time between semesters. And I could use a student assistant, if there's one available."

Canutti had leaned far back in his plastic-covered chair during the middle of this speech, as though Bryce had physically pushed him down into the soft and billowy foam cushions. "The labs are all being used, Nate," he said. "You know we've got more industrial and military projects now than we can handle. Why don't you write the company that makes the film and query them?"

He tried to keep his voice level. "I've already written them. They don't answer their mail. Nobody knows anything about them. There's nothing about them in the journals—not even

in *American Photochemistry.*" He stopped a minute. "Look, all I
need is a lab, Professor Canutti . . . I can do without the assistant."

"Walt. Walt Canutti. But the labs are full, Nate. Co-
ordinator Johnson would have me by the ruddy ears if I—"

"Look . . . Walt . . . This is *basic* research. Johnson is always
giving speeches about basic research, isn't he? The backbone of
science. All we appear to be doing here is developing cheaper
ways to make insecticides, and perfecting gas bombs."

Canutti raised his eyebrows, his chubby body still sunk in
cushioning foam. "We don't make a habit of talking about
our military projects that way, Nate. Our applied tactical
research is—"

"All right. All right." He fought his voice back down, trying
to make it sound normal. "Killing people is basic, I suppose.
Part of the nation's life, too. But this film . . ."

Canutti flushed at the sarcasm. "Look, Nate," he said, "what
you want to do is diddle with a commercial process. And,
moreover, one that already works just fine. Why blow your top
over it? So the film's a little unusual. All the better."

"My God," he said, "this film is more than unusual. You can
see that. You're a chemist—a better chemist than I am. Can't
you see the techniques this thing implies? My Lord, barium
salts and a gaseous developer!" He suddenly remembered the
roll of film still in his hand, and held it out as if it were a snake,
or a holy relic. "It's as if we were . . . as if we were cave-men,
scratching fleas out of our armpits, and one of us found a . . . a
roll of toy caps . . ." And then, in an instant, it struck him like
a physical blow in the chest and, pausing in his speech a second he thought, *Good holy God—that roll of caps!* ". . . and threw
them in the fire. Think of the tradition, the technical tradition,

that went into making a strip of paper with little gunpowder pods in a neat row, so that we could hear the little *pop, pop, pop!* Or if you gave an ancient Roman a wrist-watch, and he knew what a sundial was . . ." He didn't finish the comparison, thinking now of that roll of caps, how they had gone off so loudly, had not smelled of gunpowder at all.

Canutti smiled coldly. "Well, Nate, you're very eloquent. But I wouldn't get so worked up over a thing that some hot research team thought up." He tried to sound humorous, to joke away the disagreement. "I doubt we've been visited by men of the future. Not, at least, to sell us camera film."

Bryce stood up, clenching the film box in his hand. He spoke softly, "Hot research team, the devil! And for all I know—the way this film doesn't use a single chemical technique from over a hundred years of development in photography—this process might be extraterrestrial. Or there's a genius hiding somewhere in Kentucky who's going to be selling us perpetual motion machines next week." Abruptly, he turned, sick of the interview, and began walking toward the door.

Like a mother calling after a child who leaves in a tantrum, Canutti said, "I wouldn't talk about extraterrestrial too much, Nate. Of course, I understand what you mean . . ."

"Of course you do," Bryce said, leaving.

He went directly home on the afternoon monorail, and began looking—or, rather, listening—for small boys with cap guns . . .

CHAPTER SIX

FIVE MINUTES AFTER he left the airport he realized that he had made a serious mistake. He should not have attempted to come this far south in the summer-time, no matter how necessary it was. He could have sent Farnsworth, sent someone, to buy property, to make arrangements. The temperature was over ninety and, being physically unable to perspire, his body having been designed for temperatures in the forties, he was sick almost to unconsciousness in the backseat of the airport limousine that drove him, grinding his still gravity-sensitive body against its hard cushions, into downtown Louisville.

But, in more than two years on Earth and with the ten years of physical conditioning he had undergone before leaving Anthea, he was able to endure the pain and keep himself, by force of will, grimly, although confusedly, conscious. He was able to get from the limousine into the hotel lobby, and from the lobby up the elevator—relieved that it was a smooth-running, slow elevator—and into his third-floor room, where he fell on the bed the moment the bellboy had left him to himself. After a moment he managed to get to the air-conditioner and set it for very cold. Then he fell back on the bed. It was a good air-conditioner; it was based on a group of patents he had leased to the company that made it. In a short while the room became sufficiently comfortable for him, but he left the machine on, thankful that his contribution to the science of refrigeration had managed to make the ugly little boxes, so necessary to him, noiseless.

It was noon, and after a while he called room service and had a bottle of Chablis and some cheese sent up to him. He had only recently begun drinking wine, pleased to find that it had, apparently, the same effect on him as it did on men of Earth. The wine was good, although the cheese was a little rubbery. He turned on the television set, which also operated on W. E. Corp. patents, and settled back in an armchair, determined, if he could do nothing else this hot afternoon, to enjoy himself.

It had been over a year since he had watched television at any length, and it seemed very strange to him, here in this plush and vulgarly modern hotel suite—so much like the apartments in which television private detectives lived, with its lounge chairs, never-used bookshelves, abstract paintings and plastic-topped private bar—here in Louisville, Kentucky, to be watching again. Watching the little human men and women moving about on the screen as he had watched them for so many years at home, on Anthea. He thought of those days now, sipping the cool wine, nibbling cheese—foreign, strange foods—while the background music of a love story filled the cool room and the dimly heard voices from the little speaker sounded against his sensitive, otherworld hearing like the alien gutturals and gibberings that, fundamentally, they were. So much unlike the purring of his own language, even though the one had, ages ago, developed from the other. He permitted himself to think, for the first time in months, of the soft conversation of old Anthean friends, of the mild and brittle foods that he had eaten all his life at home, and of his wife and children. Perhaps it was the coolness of the room, calming him after his excruciating summer trip, perhaps the alcohol, still new to his veins, that made him fall into a state of mind so closely resembling human nostalgia—sentimental, self-regarding and bitter. He wanted, suddenly, to hear the sound of his language being spoken, to see the light colors of Anthean soil, to smell the acrid desert odor, to hear the thick sounds of Anthean music, and to see the thin, gauze-like walls of its buildings, the dust of its cities. And he wanted his wife, with the dim Anthean body sexuality—a quiet, insistent aching. And, suddenly, looking again at his room, at its discreet gray walls and its vulgar furniture, he felt disgusted, weary of this cheap and alien place, this loud, throaty, rootless, and sensual culture, this aggregate of clever, itchy, self-absorbed apes—vulgar, uncaring, while their flimsy civilization was, like London Bridge and all bridges, falling down, falling down.

He began to feel what he had sometimes felt before: a heavy lassitude, a world-weariness, a profound fatigue with this busy, busy, destructive world and all its chittering noises. He felt as though he could give the whole thing up, that it was foolish, impossibly foolish to have started it, more than twenty years before. He looked around him again, tiredly. What was he doing here—here on this other world, third from the sun, a hundred million miles from his home? He got up and turned the television set off, and then sat back deeply in the chair, still drinking the wine, feeling the alcohol now and not caring.

He had watched American, British, and Russian television for fifteen years. His colleagues had collected a huge library of monitored and recorded television broadcasts, and by the time, forty years ago, when America had begun continuous television broadcasting, they had already deciphered most of the subtleties of the language from FM radio broadcasts. He had studied daily, learning the language, the manners, the history and geography, everything available, until he had memorized, by means of exhaustive cross-referencing, the meaning of obscure words like "yellow," "Waterloo," and "Democratic Republic"—the last a thing which had no counterpart whatever on Anthea. And, while he had worked and studied and done endless physical exercises, while he agonized in anticipation for years, they had deliberated, deciding whether the trip should even be attempted. There was so little power, other than the solar batteries in the desert. It would require so much fuel to send even one Anthean across the empty gulf, possibly to his death, possibly to be received by an already dead world, a world that might by then be, like so much of Anthea itself, littered with atomic rubble, the burned-out residue of ape-like wrath. But they had told him, finally, that the trip would be attempted, in one of the old, old craft that still remained underground. He was informed a year before the journey that the plans at last were definite, that the ship would be ready when the planets had assumed the right position for the crossing. He had not been able to control the trembling of his hands, when he had told his wife of the decision . . .

———

He waited in his hotel room, not moving from the chair, until five o'clock. Then he got up, called the real estate office, and told them they could expect him at five-thirty. He left the room, leaving the half-empty bottle of wine on the bar. He hoped that the weather would be much cooler by then, but it was not.

He had chosen the hotel because it was within three blocks of the office he was going to visit, the office where he was to begin the huge real estate transaction he had already planned. He was able to walk the distance; but the sullen, heavy and agonizingly hot air that seemed to cover the streets like a cushion made him dizzy, confused and weak. For a few moments he thought he should return to the hotel and have the real estate men come to him, but he kept on walking.

And then, when he found the building, he discovered a thing that frightened him: the office he wanted was on the nineteenth floor. He had not expected tall buildings in Kentucky, had not anticipated this. Walking up the stairs was out of the question. And he did not know anything about the elevators. If he should ride in one that went up too fast, or jerked, it might be disastrous to his already gravity-strained body. But the elevators looked new and well made, and, at least, the building was air-conditioned. He stepped into one, empty except for the operator, a quiet-looking old man with a tobacco-stained uniform. They took on one more passenger, a chubby, pretty woman who came running up, breathless, at the last moment. Then the operator closed the brass doors, Newton said, "Nineteen, please," the woman muttered "twelve," and the old man lazily, somewhat contemptuously, placed his hand on the manual control handle. Newton realized instantly, in dismay, that this was not a modern, push-button elevator, but some kind of refurbished old one. But this realization was a moment too late, for, before he could protest, he felt his stomach twist and his muscles tighten in pain as the elevator jerked, hesitated, jerked again and then shot upward, doubling, for a moment, his already trebled weight. And then everything seemed to happen at once. He saw the woman staring at him and knew that his nose must be bleeding, pouring blood on his shirt front, and looking down saw that this was so. At the same instant he heard—or felt, in his quivering body—a brittle cracking, and his legs collapsed under him and he fell to the floor of the elevator, grotesquely twisted, seeing one leg horribly jack-knifed under him as he lost consciousness, his mind falling into a blackness as profound as that of the void that separated him from his home . . .

He had been unconscious twice before in his life: once during the training in the centrifuge at home, and once during the blind acceleration of his take-off in the ship. Both of those times he had recovered himself quickly, coming awake to confusion and pain. This time, too, he awoke to the aching of an abused body and the frightened confusion of not knowing where he was. He was lying on his back, on something smooth and soft, and there were bright lights in his eyes. He squinted and then winced, turning his head. He was lying on some kind of couch. On the other side of the room, a woman was standing at a desk, holding a telephone in her hand. She was looking at him. He stared at her, and then realized who she was—the woman from the elevator.

She hesitated, seeing him awaken, and did not seem to know what to do with the telephone, holding it limply in her hand. She smiled at him vaguely. "You all right, mister?"

His voice sounded like someone else's, weak and soft. "I believe so. I don't know . . ." His legs were stretched out in front of him. He was afraid to try to move them. The blood on his shirt was still sticky, but cold now. He could not have been unconscious long. "I believe I hurt my legs . . ."

She looked at him gravely, shaking her head. "You sure did. One of 'em bent up like old baling wire."

He kept looking at her, not knowing what to say, trying to think of what he should do. He could not go to a hospital; there would be an examination, X-rays . . .

"I been trying to get you a doctor for five minutes." Her voice was hoarse and she looked frightened. "I already called three and they're not in."

He blinked at her, trying to think clearly. "No," he said. "No! Don't call . . ."

"Don't call a doctor? But you got to have a doctor, mister. You been bad hurt." She looked doubtful, worried, but too frightened to be suspicious.

"No." He tried to say more, but was suddenly overcome with nausea and, hardly aware of what he was doing, found himself vomiting over the side of the couch, his legs screaming with pain at each convulsion. Then, exhausted, he lay back again, face up. But the lights were too bright, burning his eyes even through the closed lids—his thin, translucent eyelids—and, groaning, he threw his arm up, to cover them.

Somehow, his being sick seemed to calm her. Perhaps it was the recognizable humanness of the act. Her voice was more easy. "Can I help?" she said. "Is there something I can do to help?" She hesitated. "I can get you a drink . . ."

"No. I don't want . . ." *What was he going to do?*

Suddenly her voice got light, as though she had been near hysteria and had just drawn back from it. "You sure are a mess," she said.

"I imagine." He turned his face toward the back of the couch, trying to avoid the lights. "Can you . . . can you just leave me alone? I'll be better . . . if I can rest."

She laughed softly. "I don't see how. This here's an office; there's going to be people filling it up in the morning. The elevator boy gave me the key."

"Oh." He had to do something about the pain, or he would not stay conscious long. "Listen," he said, "I have a hotel key in my pocket, the Brown Hotel. It's three blocks from here, down the street you take as—"

"I know where the Brown Hotel is."

"Oh. That's fine. Can you take the key and get a black brief-case from the bedroom closet in the room? And bring it to me? I have . . . medicine in it. Please."

She was silent.

"I can pay you . . ."

"That's not what I'm worried about." He turned and opened his eyes to look at her a moment. Her broad face was frowning, the eyebrows wrinkled in a kind of parody of deep thought. Then she laughed loosely, not looking at him. "I don't know as they'd let me in the Brown Hotel—or let me walk into one of the rooms, like I owned it."

"Why not?" It hurt him somewhere in his chest to talk. He felt as though he would faint again before long. "Why can't you?"

"You don't know much about clothes, do you, mister? You look like you never had to worry. I ain't wearing nothing but a country dress, and that torn. And they might not like my breath."

"Oh!" he said.

"Gin. But maybe I could . . ." She looked thoughtful. "No, I couldn't."

He felt himself going watery again, his body felt as if he were floating. Blinking, he forced himself to hold on, trying to ignore the weakness, the pain. "In my billfold. Get the twenty-dollar bills. Give the bellboys the money. You can do it." The room was spinning about him, the lights going fainter now, seeming to move in dim procession, across his vision. "Please."

He felt her fumbling in his pocket, felt her hot breath on his face, then, after a moment, heard her gasp. "Lordy!" she said, "if you ain't loaded . . . ! Why, I could run off with this."

"Don't," he said. "Please help me. I'm rich. I can . . ."

"I won't," she said wearily. And then, more brightly, "You just hang on, mister. I'll get back with your medicine, if I have to buy the hotel. You just take it easy."

He heard her closing the door behind her as he fainted . . .

It seemed only a moment later that she was back in the room, panting, and had the briefcase open, on the desk.

And then, after he had taken the pain capsules and the pills that would help to heal his leg, the elevator operator came in with a man who said he was building superintendent and Newton had to reassure them that he would sue no one, that, really, he felt fine and that all would be well. No, he did not need an ambulance. Yes, he would sign a waiver to absolve the building of responsibility. Now would they get him to a taxi? He almost fainted again, several times, during this frenetic discussion, and when it was over he did faint again.

He awoke in a taxi with the woman. She was shaking him gently. "Where do you want to go?" She said, "Where's your home?"

He stared at her. "I . . . I don't really know."

CHAPTER SEVEN

HE LOOKED UP from his reading, somewhat startled. He had not known she was in the room. She frequently did that, seemed to appear from nowhere, and her hoarse, serious voice could be irritating to him. But she was a good woman, and entirely unsuspicious. In four weeks he had grown very fond of her, as if she were a kind of useful pet. He shifted his leg to a more comfortable position before he answered. "You'll be going to church this afternoon, won't you?" He looked over his shoulder at her. She must have just come in; she was carrying a red plastic grocery sack, hugging it against her heavy bosom as if it were a child.

She grinned at him a little foolishly, and he realized that she was probably already somewhat drunk, even though it was early afternoon. "That's what I mean, Mr. Newton. I thought you might want to go to church." She set the sack on the table by the air-conditioner—the one he had bought for her during his first week at her home. "I got you some wine," she said.

He turned back toward his leg, propped up in front of him on a flimsy little crate that was weighed down with old comic books, her only reading material. He was annoyed. Her buying wine meant that she definitely intended to get drunk that evening, and, although she held her liquor well, he was always made apprehensive by her drunkenness. Even though she commented often and with amused wonder upon his lightness and frailty, she probably still had no idea of the harm she could do his frame—his slight, bird-like bones—if she were ever to stumble over him, fall on him, or even merely slap him hard. She was a sturdy, fleshy woman, and outweighed him by at least fifty pounds. "It was thoughtful of you to bring the wine, Betty Jo," he said. "Is it chilled?"

"Uh huh," she said. "Too damn cold, in fact." She took the bottle from the sack, and he heard it clink against other, still hidden, companions. She felt of it speculatively. "I didn't buy it at Reichmann's this time. Today was my day for the welfare check, and I just got it as I come out of the welfare building. There's a little store there called Goldie's Quickie. Gets a lot of the welfare business." She took a tumbler from a row of them that sat on top of the ancient, red-painted bookshelf and set it on the window ledge. Then, with the kind of lazy abstraction that characterized her dealings with liquor, she pulled a bottle of gin from the sack, and stood now, a wine bottle in one hand, a bottle of gin in the other, as if undecided which to set down first. "They keep all the wine in a regular refrigerator, and it gets too cold. I should of bought it over at Reichmann's." She finally set the wine bottle down, and opened the gin.

"That's all right," he said. "It shouldn't take long to warm up."

"I'll just set it here, and just any time you want some you ask me, hear?" She poured herself a half tumbler of the gin and then went into the little kitchen. He heard her clinking the sugar bowl, spooning in the sugar that she always put in her gin, and then she returned in a minute, drinking as she walked. "Damn, I like gin!" she said, in a self-satisfied tone.

"I don't believe I'll be able to go to church."

She looked genuinely disappointed. She came over and sat awkwardly in the aged chintz-covered chair that faced his, pulling her print skirt over her knees with one hand while she held the glass with the other. "I'm sorry. It's a real good church, and high-class too. You wouldn't be out of place at all." He noticed for the first time that she was wearing a diamond ring. She had probably bought it with his money. He did not begrudge it to her; she had certainly earned it by the care she had taken of him. In spite of her habits and her talk, she was an excellent nurse. And she wasn't curious about him.

Not wanting to talk further about the church, he remained silent while she settled herself comfortably in the chair and began working seriously on her gin. She was the sort of irregular and sentimental churchgoer whom television interviewers would call deeply religious—she claimed that her religion was a great source of strength. It consisted largely of attending Sunday afternoon lectures about personal magnetism and Wednesday evening lectures about men who became successful in business through prayer. Its faith was based on a belief that whatever happened, all would be well; its morality was that each must decide for himself what was right for him. Betty Jo apparently had decided on gin and relief, as had a great many others.

In a few weeks of living with this woman he had learned a great deal about one aspect of American society that television had not informed him of at all. He had known about the general prosperity that had bloomed continuously, like the flower of some giant and impossibly hardy weed, for the forty years since the end of World War II, and he had known how this wealth had been distributed among and spent by the nearly all-inclusive middle class that, as every year passed, put more time into less productive work and made more money for it. It was that overdressed and immensely comfortable middle class that almost all television shows dealt with, so that one could easily get the notion that all Americans were young, suntanned, clear-eyed and ambitious. In meeting Betty Jo he had learned that there was a large substratum of society that was totally unaffected by this middle-class prototype, that a huge and indifferent mass of persons had virtually no ambitions and no values whatever. He had read enough history to realize that people like Betty Jo would once have been the industrial poor; but they were now the industrial well-to-do, living comfortably in government-built housing—Betty Jo rented a three-room dwelling unit in a huge old brick housing project, now a semi-slum—on checks from a bewildering diversity of agencies: Federal Welfare, State Welfare, Emergency Relief, Country Poor Relief. This American society was so rich that it could support the eight or ten million members of Betty Jo's class in a kind of shabby, gin-and-used-furniture luxury in the cities, while the bulk of the country tanned its healthy cheeks by its suburban swimming pools and followed the current fashions in clothes and child-rearing and mixed drinks and wives, playing endless games with religion and psycho-analysis and "creative leisure." With the exception of Farnsworth, who belonged to still another, rarer class, that of the genuinely wealthy, all of the men whom Newton had met were of this middle class. All of them were very much alike and seeming, if you caught them off their guard, when the hand wasn't extended in friendliness or the face composed in its usual mask of smug and boyish charm, a little haggard, a little lost. It seemed to Newton that Betty Jo, with her gin, her boredom, her cats and her used furniture, was getting the better part of the social arrangement.

She had had a party once, with some "girl friends" from other units in the building. He had remained in the bedroom out of sight, but he had been able to hear them well enough, singing old hymns like *Rock of Ages* and *Faith of Our Fathers*, and getting drunk on gin and sentimentality, and it had seemed to him that they had found a better kind of satisfaction in this emotional debauch than the middle class derived from its Roman barbecue feasts, its drunken midnight swimming and its quick sex. Yet even Betty Jo was false to those childish old hymns, for after the other women had gone drunkenly back to their own three-room cells, she had laid by him in bed and giggled about the silliness of the Baptist, hymn-singing, revivalist religion that her Kentucky family had brought her up in and how she had "outgrown all that, even though, sometimes, it was kind of cute to sing the songs." Newton said nothing to this, yet he could not help but wonder. He had seen an "old-time revival hour" several times, on the old Anthean TV tapes, and he had seen a "modern" church hour which "made a creative use of God," for which the music consisted solely of an electronic organ playing Strauss waltzes and parts of *The Poet and Peasant Overture*. He was not at all certain that these people had been entirely wise in their development of that strange manifestation of theirs, a thing Anthea was totally without—and yet which the Antheans, in their ancient visits to the planet, were probably to blame for—this peculiar set of premises and promises called religion. He did not understand it very well, however. Antheans believed, to be sure, that there probably were gods in the universe, or creatures that might be called gods, but this was not a thing of any great importance to them, any more than it really was to most humans. Yet the old human belief in sin and redemption was meaningful to him and he, like all Antheans, was quite familiar with the sense of guilt and the need for its expiation. Yet now the humans seemed to be building loose constructions of half-belief and sentiment to replace their religions, and he did not know what to make of it; he could not really fathom why Betty Jo was so much concerned over the supposed strength she received in weekly doses from her synthetic church, a form of strength that seemed less certain and more troublesome than that she received from her gin.

After a while he asked her for a glass of wine, which she obligingly got for him, handing him the one little crystal wine glass that she had bought especially for him and then pouring expertly from the bottle. He drank it off rather quickly. He had learned to enjoy alcohol considerably, during his convalescence.

"Well," he said, as she was pouring the second glass for him, "I expect I'll be able to move from here next week."

She hesitated a moment and then finished pouring the wine. Then she said, "What for, Tommy?" She called him Tommy sometimes when she was getting drunk. "There's no call to hurry."

CHAPTER EIGHT

LORD, HE WAS peculiar. Tall and skinny and wide-eyed like a bird; but he could move around, even with a broken leg, like a cat. He took pills all the time and he never shaved. He didn't seem to sleep either; she would get up sometimes at night, waking up with the dry throat and spinning head that the gin would give her when she hadn't watched it too close, and there he'd be in the living room, his leg propped up, reading, or listening to that little gold record player that the fat man had brought him from New York, or just sitting in the chair with his hands under his chin, staring at the wall with his lips tight together and his mind God only could ever know where. She would try to move quietly at times like that, so as not to disturb him; but he always heard her no matter how quiet she was and she could tell he was startled. But he would always smile at her and sometimes say a word or two. Once, during the second week, he had seemed so lost and alone, sitting, staring at the wall as if he was trying to find something there that he could talk to; he looked, with his twisted leg, like some half-broken baby bird that had fallen from a nest. He was so pitiful that she felt like putting her arms around his head and stroking him, mothering him. But she hadn't done it; she already knew about how he didn't like to be touched. And he was such a light thing, she might hurt him. She would never forget how light he was when she carried him off that elevator the first time, with the blood on his shirt and his leg twisted like a bent wire.

She finished brushing her hair, and then began putting on lipstick. She used, for the first time, some of the silver lipstick and eye shadow that young girls wore; and when she had finished this she looked at herself in the mirror with some pleasure. For forty she wasn't bad to look at, if you covered up the tiny purplish places around her eyes that came from gin and sugar. She was covering them up tonight, with a makeup bought just for that.

After looking at her face for a while she began to dress, putting on the sheer gold panties and brassiere that she'd bought that afternoon, and then the crimson pants and the matching blouse. Garish earrings, and finally the silver flakes in her hair. She looked now like somebody else and, standing before the mirror, she at first felt self-conscious. What kind of foolishness was she up to, dressing like this? But, in the back of her mind, in that vague, seldom-examined registry where bottles of gin were mercilessly numbered and unpleasant recollections of a thankfully dead husband were filed, she knew perfectly well what she was doing this for. But she did not bring it to the surface of her mind to inspect it. She was expert at the technique. In a minute she felt more accustomed to this new, sexy-matron appearance, and, taking her tumbler of gin from the top of the dresser in one hand, smoothing the tight crimson pants with the other, she pushed open the door and walked into the room where Tommy was sitting.

He was on the phone, and she could see the face of that lawyer, Farnsworth, on the little screen. They usually talked three or four times a day, and once Farnsworth had come with a staff of earnest-looking young men, and they had spent the day discussing and arguing in her living room, ignoring her as if she'd been a part of the furniture. Except for Tommy, that is, because he had been polite and nice and had thanked her gently when she had brought the men coffee and offered them gin.

She sat on the couch while he talked to Farnsworth and picked up an old comic book and lazily looked over some of the more sexy pages while she finished the drink. But this bored her, and Tommy was still talking about some kind of research project that they were doing in the southern part of the state and about selling shares of this and that. She set the comic book down, finished her drink, picked up one of his books that sat on the end table. He'd had hundreds of books sent to the house, and the room was getting crowded with them. The book turned out to be some kind of poetry and she put it back hastily, picking up another. It was called *Thermonuclear Engines* and was filled with lines and numbers. She began to feel silly again, dressed in these clothes. She got up and resolutely fixed two drinks of gin, leaving one on top of the television set and taking the other back to the couch with her. Yet, silly as she felt, she found herself automatically taking a seductive, movie-star pose on the couch, and stretching her heavy legs out lazily. She watched him over the top of her glass, saw the glow of the lamplight on his white hair and on his delicate, brownish, almost transparent skin, and then his graceful, womanish hand that lay casually, lightly on the desk. At that moment she began consciously to review what she was up to and, in the soft light, with the gin warming her stomach, she began to feel a touch of wicked excitement in her from flirting at the edge of the idea of that strange, delicate body against hers. Looking at him and letting her imagination play with the thought, she knew that the particular thrill came from his strangeness—his strange, un-manlike, unsexual nature. Maybe she was like those women who like to make love with freaks and cripples. Well, he was both—and she did not care now, was not ashamed, with the tight pants on and the gin in her. If she could arouse him—if he could be aroused—she would be proud of herself. And if not—he was a dear man anyway and he wouldn't be offended. She felt her heart go out to him then in quick, warm sentiment; as she finished her drink she felt, for the first time in years, an emotion resembling love, along with the desire that she had been working herself up to all day long—since this morning when she had gone out in her aged print dress and bought panties and earrings, makeup and tights, without admitting to herself the final meaning of the vague plan that had entered her mind.

She got still another drink, telling herself that she ought to go easy. But she was getting nervous, waiting. He was talking now about somebody named Bryce and Farnsworth was saying that this Bryce was trying to see him, wanted to come to work for them, but wanted to see Tommy first, and Tommy was saying it was impossible and Farnsworth was saying they needed all the men they could get with Bryce's training. She began to be impatient. Who cared about this Bryce? But then, abruptly, Tommy ended the conversation, hung up the phone, and after remaining silent for a minute looked over at her, smiling thoughtfully. "My new place is ready, down in the southern part of the state. Would you like to go there with me? As my housekeeper?"

Well that was a shock. She blinked at him. "Housekeeper?"

"Yes. The house will be ready Saturday, but there will be furniture to arrange, things of that sort to take care of. I'll need someone to help with it all. And," he smiled, getting up with his cane and limping over toward her, "you know I dislike meeting strangers. You could talk to people for me." He stood up over her.

She blinked up at him. "I fixed you a drink. On the television." His offer was hard to believe. She had known about the house from when the real estate people had come by that second week—a huge old mansion that he was buying, and nine hundred acres of land, down east in the mountains.

He picked up the glass, sniffed it, and said, "Gin?"

"I thought you ought to try it," she said. "It's pretty good. Sweet."

"No," he said. "No. But I'll be glad to have some wine with you."

"Sure, Tommy." She got up, staggering a bit, and went to the kitchen for his bottle of Sauterne and his crystal glass. "You don't need me," she called, from the kitchen.

His voice was solemn. "Why yes I do, Betty Jo."

She came back in, standing close to him as she handed him the glass. He was such a nice man. She felt almost ashamed of herself wanting to seduce him, as though he were a baby. She could not help being drunkenly amused. He probably didn't know what it was all about. He was the kind that probably peed in a silver pot when he was little and ran away if a girl tried to touch him. Or maybe he was queer—anybody who sat around reading all the time and looked like he did . . . But he didn't talk like a queer. She liked to hear him talk. He looked tired now. But he looked tired all the time.

He sat down, painfully, in the armchair, and set his cane on the floor beside him. She sat on the couch and then lay back on her side, facing him. He was looking at her but he hardly seemed to see her. When he looked that way it made her feel creepy. "I'm wearing new clothes," she said.

"So you are."

"Yeah. So I am." She laughed self-consciously. "The pants was sixty-five and the blouse was fifty, and I bought gold undies and earrings." She raised a leg to show off the bright red pants and then scratched her knee through the cloth. "With the money you been giving me I could dress like a movie star if I wanted to. I could get my face fixed, you know, and take off weight and all." She felt her earrings for a minute, thoughtfully, tugging at them and running her thumbnail across the soft, metallic gold, enjoying the little hints of pain on her earlobes. "But I don't know. I been sloppy a long time. Ever since me and Barney went on welfare and medicare and all I let myself go and, hell, you get so you like it that way."

He said nothing for a while and they sat in silence while she finished her drink. Finally he said, "Will you come with me to the new house?"

She stretched and yawned, beginning to feel tired. "You sure you really need me?"

For a moment he blinked at her and his face looked a way she had never seen it look before, as if he were pleading with her. "Yes, I do need you," he said. "I know very few people . . ."

"Sure," she said. "I'll come." She gestured tiredly. "I'd be a damn fool not to, anyway, since I imagine you'll pay me twice as much as I'm worth."

"Good." His face relaxed a little and he settled back in his chair and picked up a book.

Before he could get started in it she recalled her plans, already cool by now, and after a moment of reluctant doubt she made a final try. But she was sleepy and her heart wasn't in it. "Are you married, Tommy?" she asked. It should have been a pretty obvious question.

If he had any idea of what she was driving at he didn't show it. "Yes, I'm married," he said, politely putting his book in his lap and looking over at her.

Embarrassed, she said, "I just wanted to know." And then, "What does she look like? Your wife."

"Oh, she resembles me, I imagine. Tall and thin."

Somehow her embarrassment was turning into irritation. She finished off her drink and said, "I used to be thin," almost with defiance. Then, tired of it, she stood up and walked over to her bedroom door. The whole thing had been silly anyway. And maybe he was queer—being married didn't prove anything that way. Anyway he was peculiar. A nice, rich man, but weird as green milk. Still irritated she said, "Good night," and went into her room and began peeling off her expensive clothes. Then she sat on the edge of the bed a moment, in her nightgown, thinking. She was much more comfortable with the tight clothes off, and when she finally lay down, her mind now blank, she had no difficulty in falling into a deep sleep, pleasantly filled with undisturbing dreams.

CHAPTER NINE

THEY FLEW OVER mountains, but the little plane was so stable, the pilot so expert, that there was no pitching, almost no sensation of movement. They flew over Harlan, Kentucky, a drab city sprawled loosely in the foothills, and then over vast, barren fields and down into a valley. Bryce, a glass of whisky in his hand, saw the distant gleam of a lake, its static surface shining like a new and rich coin; and then they dipped lower, losing sight of the lake, and landed on a broad, new strip of concrete that sat at the flat bottom of the valley, amid broom straw and upturned red clay, like a wild Euclidian diagram drawn there with gray chalk by some geometrically minded god.

Bryce stepped from the plane into the thumping din of earth-moving machinery, the confusion of khaki-shirted men, red-faced in the summer heat, shouting hoarsely at one another, in the process of building unidentifiable buildings. There were machinery sheds, some kind of huge concrete platform, a row of barracks. For a moment, having left the quiet and coolness of the smooth, air-conditioned plane—Thomas Jerome New-ton's personal plane, sent to Louisville for him—he was bewil-dered, made dizzy by heat and noise, by all this feverish and unexplained activity.

A young man, rugged looking as a cigarette advertisement, stepped up to him. The man wore a pith helmet; his rolled-up sleeves displayed an abundance of tanned, youthful muscle; he looked exactly like a hero of one of those half-forgotten boys' novels that had, at a dimly remembered time of aspir-ing adolescence, made him, Bryce, dedicated to becoming an engineer—a chemical engineer, a man of science and of action. He did not smile at the young man, thinking of his own paunch, his graying hair, and the taste of whisky in his mouth; but he nodded his head in recognition.

The man held out a hand. "You're Professor Bryce?"

He took the hand, expecting an affectedly firm grip, pleased to receive a gentle one. "Professor no more," he said, "but I'm Bryce."

"Good. Good. I'm Hopkins. Foreman." The man's friend-liness seemed dog-like, as if he were pleading for approval. "What do you think of it all, Doctor Bryce?" He gestured toward the rows of buildings going up. Just beyond them was a tall tower, apparently a broadcasting antenna of some kind.

Bryce cleared his throat. "I don't know." He started to ask what they were making here, but decided that his ignorance would be embarrassing. Why hadn't that fat buffoon, Farns-worth, told him what he was being hired for? "Is Mr. Newton expecting me?" he said aloud, not looking at the man.

"Sure. Sure." Suddenly showing efficiency, the young man hustled him around to the other side of the plane, where a small monorail car, obscured before, sat atop a dully gleaming track that snaked away into the hills at the side of the valley like a thin, silvery pencil line. Hopkins slid the door back, revealing polished leather upholstery and a satisfyingly dark interior. "This'll have you up at the house in five minutes."

"The house? How far is it?"

"About four miles. I'll call ahead and Brinnarde'll meet you. Brinnarde's Mr. Newton's secretary; he'll probably do the interviewing."

Bryce hesitated before getting into the car. "Won't I meet Mr. Newton?" The thought upset him; after these two years, not to meet the man who had invented Worldcolor, who operated the biggest oil refineries in Texas, who had developed three-D television, reusable photo negatives, the ATF process in dye-transfer—the man who was either the world's most original inventive genius, or an extraterrestrial.

The young man frowned. "I doubt it. I've been here six months and I've never seen him, except from behind the window of that car you're getting into. About once a week he comes down here in it, to look things over, I guess. But he never gets out, and it's so dark inside that you can't see his face, only the shadow of it, looking out."

Bryce settled himself into the car. "Doesn't he ever get out?" He nodded toward the plane, where a group of mechanics, seeming to have come from nowhere, were beginning to go over the jets. "To fly . . . places?"

Hopkins grinned, inanely, it seemed to Bryce. "Only at night, and you can't see him then. He's a tall man, though, and thin. The pilot's told me that; but that's about all. The pilot isn't much of a talker."

"I see." He touched the door button and the door slid back, noiselessly. As it was shutting, Hopkins said, "Good luck!" and he replied quickly, "Thank you," but was not sure whether or not his voice had been cut off by the door.

Like the plane, the car was soundproof and very cool. Also like the plane, it began moving with almost imperceptible acceleration, gathering speed so smoothly that there was little sensation of motion. He lightened the transparency of the windows by turning the little silver knob that was obviously for that purpose, and watched the frail-looking aluminum construction sheds, and the groups of working men—an unusual and, he felt, satisfactory sight, in these days of automatic factories and six-hour working days. The men seemed eager, working heartily, sweating under the Kentucky sun. It occurred to him that they must be very well paid to have come to this barren place, so far from golf courses, municipal gambling halls and other consolations of the working man. He saw one young man—so many of them seemed young—sitting atop a huge earth-mover, grinning with the pleasure of pushing great quantities of mud; for a moment Bryce envied him his work and his young, unquestioning confidence, easy under the hot sun.

A moment later he had left the construction site and was threading through densely foliated hills, moving so fast now that the trees close to him were a blur of sunlight and green leaves, of light and shadow. He leaned back, against the extraordinarily comfortable cushions, trying to enjoy the ride. But he was too excited to relax, too keyed up by the speed of events and all of the excitement of a strange, new place—so blissfully far, now, from Iowa, from college students, bearded intellectuals, men like Canutti. He looked toward the windows, watching the increasingly rapid flashing of light, shade,

light, pale green and dark shadows; and then, abruptly ahead of
him, as the car sped over a rise, he saw the glimmer of the lake,
spread out in a hollow like a sheet of wonderfully blue-gray
metal, a giant, serene disc. Just beyond it rose, in the shadow of
a mountain, a huge, old white house with a white-columned
porch and large, shuttered windows, sitting quietly at the edge
of the broad lake, solidly, at the base of a mountain. Then the
house and lake, seen in the distance, vanished behind another
hill as the monorail track dipped down, and he realized that
the car was beginning to decelerate. A minute later the house
and lake reappeared and the car eased in a broad, curving glide
that swooped along the edge of the water, delicately inclining
with the curve of the track, and he saw a man standing, waiting
for him, at the side of the house. The car came to a gentle stop
and Bryce took a deep breath, touched the doorknob, watched
the wood-paneled door slide quietly open, and stepped out
into the shade of the mountain and the smell of pine trees and
the gentle, almost inaudible sound of water lapping against
the shore of the lake. The man was small and dark, with little
bright eyes and a mustache. He stepped forward, smiling for-
mally. "Doctor Bryce?" His accent was French.

Suddenly feeling exhilarated, he answered, "Monsieur Brinnarde?" holding out his hand to the man. *"Enchanté."*

The man took his hand, his eyebrows slightly raised. *"Soyez
le bienvenu, Monsieur le Docteur. Monsieur Newton vous attend.
Alors . . ."*

Bryce caught his breath. "Newton will see me?"

"Yes. I will show you the way."

Inside the house he was greeted by three cats, who stared
at him from the floor where they had been playing. They

seemed to be ordinary alley cats, but well fed, and scornful of his entrance. He did not like cats. The Frenchman led him silently through the parlor and up a heavily carpeted staircase. There were pictures on the walls—odd, expensive-looking tableaux by painters he did not recognize. The staircase was very wide, and curved. He noticed that it had one of those motor-powered seats, folded now, that could run up and down by the banister. Could Newton be a cripple? There seemed to be no one else in the house except the two of them, and the cats. He glanced back; they were still staring at him, eyes wide, curious and insolent.

At the top of the stairs was a hall, and at the end of the hall was a door, which obviously led into Newton's room. It opened and a rather sad-eyed, plump woman came out, wearing an apron. She walked up to them, blinked at him and said, "I guess you're Professor Bryce." Her voice, amiable and throaty, was thick with a hill-billy accent.

He nodded and she led him to the door. He walked in alone, noticing to his dismay that his breath was short and his legs unsteady.

The room was immense and the air in it was cold. The light came dimly from a huge, only slightly transparent bay window that overlooked the lake. There seemed to be furniture everywhere, in a bewildering array of colors—the heavy forms of couches, a table, desks, taking on blues and grays and faded orange as his eyes became accustomed to the dim, yellowish light. Two pictures faced him on the back wall: one was an etching of a giant bird, a heron or whooping crane; the other a nervous abstraction by someone like Klee. Maybe it was a Klee. The two works did not go well together. In the corner was a giant birdcage, with a purple and red parrot, apparently asleep.

And now walking toward him slowly, carrying a cane, was a tall, thin man, with indistinct features. "Professor Bryce?" The voice was clear, faintly accented, pleasant.

"Yes. You're . . . Mr. Newton?"

"That's right. Why don't we sit down and talk for a while?"

He sat, and they talked for several minutes. Newton was pleasant, easy, a shade over-correct in his manner, but neither imposing nor snobbish. He had a great deal of natural dignity, and he discussed the painting that Bryce mentioned—it was a Klee after all—with interest and intelligence. In talking about it he stood up for a minute to point out a detail and Bryce got his first good look at the man's face. It was a fine face, beautifully featured, almost womanish, with a strange cast to it. Immediately the thought, the absurd thought that he had toyed with for over a year, came to him strongly. For a moment, watching the strange, tall man pointing a delicate finger toward an eerie, nervous-lined painting there in the dim light, it did not seem at all absurd. Yet it was; and, when Newton turned back to him, smiled, and said, "I think we ought to have a drink, Professor Bryce," the illusion vanished completely and Bryce's reason asserted itself. There were stranger-looking men than this one in the world, and there had been brilliant inventors before.

"I'd like a drink," he said. And then, "I know you're busy."

"Not at all." Newton smiled easily, walking over toward the door. "Not today at least. What would you like?"

"Scotch." He started to add, "if you have it," but checked himself. He imagined Newton would have it. "Scotch and water."

Instead of pressing a button or ringing a gong—in this house ringing a gong would not have seemed out of place— Newton merely opened the door and called out, "Betty Jo."

When she answered, he said, "Bring Professor Bryce the Scotch, with water and ice. I'd like my gin and bitters." Then he closed the door and returned to his chair. "I've only recently come to enjoy gin," he said. Bryce shuddered inwardly at the thought of gin and bitters.

"Well, Professor Bryce, what do you think of our site here? I suppose you saw all the . . . activity when you got off the plane?"

He settled back in his chair, feeling more at ease now. Newton seemed very gracious, genuinely interested in hearing what he had to say. "Yes. It looked very interesting. But to tell you the truth I don't know what you are building."

Newton stared for a moment, and then laughed. "Didn't Oliver tell you, in New York?"

Bryce shook his head.

"Oliver can be very secretive. I certainly didn't mean him to go that far." He smiled—and for the first time, Bryce was vaguely bothered by the smile, although he could not see precisely what it was that bothered him. "Perhaps that was why you demanded to see me?"

Apparently he only meant it lightly. "Maybe," Bryce said. "But I had other reasons as well."

"Yes." Newton started to say something, but stopped when the door opened and Betty Jo came in, carrying the bottles and pitchers on a tray. Bryce looked at her closely. She was a slightly pretty, middle-aged woman, the kind you would expect to see at a matinee or a bridge club. Yet her face was not vacant, not stupid, and there was warmth, a trace of good humor or amusement, around her eyes and in her full lips. But she was somewhat out of place as this millionaire's only visible servant. She said nothing and set the drinks down, and as she walked past him on her way out he was astonished at the unmistakable odors of liquor and perfume as she went by.

The Scotch had been freshly opened, and he fixed himself a drink with some amusement and wonder. Was this the way millionaire scientists went about things? One asks for a drink and a half-drunk servant brings a fifth? Perhaps it was the best way. The two of them poured the liquor in silence and then, after the first drink, Newton said unexpectedly, "It's a space vehicle."

Bryce blinked, not understanding what the man meant. "How's that?"

"The thing we're building here will be a space vehicle."

"Oh?" It was a surprise, but not overmuch of one. Space-probing craft, unmanned, of one sort or another were common enough ... Even the Cuban bloc had put one up a few months ago.

"Then you'll want me on metals for the frame?"

"No." Newton was sipping his drink slowly, and looking out the window as if thinking of something else. "The frame is worked out thoroughly already. I'd like you to work on the fuel-carrying systems—to find materials that can contain some of the chemicals, such as fuels and wastes and the like." He turned back to Bryce, smiling again, and Bryce realized that the smile was vaguely disquieting because of a hint of some incomprehensible weariness about it. "I'm afraid I know very little about materials—heat and acid resistance and stresses. Oliver says that you're one of the very best men for that kind of work."

"Farnsworth may be overrating me, but I know the work fairly well."

That seemed to end the subject and they were silent for a while. From the moment Newton had mentioned a space vehicle the old suspicion had, of course, returned. But with it came the obvious refutation—if Newton were, through some wild irrationality, from some other planet, he and his people would not be building space craft. That would be the one thing that they would be certain to have already. He smiled at himself, at the cheap, science fiction level of his own private discourse. If Newton were a Martian or a Venusian, he should, by all rights, be importing heat rays to fry New York or planning to disintegrate Chicago, or carrying off young girls to underground caves for otherworldly sacrifices. Betty Jo? Feeling imaginative now, from the whisky and his fatigue, he almost laughed aloud at the thought: Betty Jo, on a movie poster, with Newton in a plastic helmet, menacing her with a ray gun, a bulky, silvery gun with heavy convector fins and little bright zig-zags coming out of it. Newton was still looking distractedly out the window. He had already finished his first gin drink and had poured himself another. A drunken Martian? An extraterrestrial who drank gin and bitters?

Newton had spoken abruptly before—yet without rudeness—and he turned back and spoke abruptly again. "Why did you want to see me, Mr. Bryce?" His voice was not demanding, only curious.

The question caught him off guard, and he hesitated, pouring himself another drink to cover the pause. Then he said, "I was impressed with your work. The photographic films—color, X-ray—and your innovations in electronic gear. I thought them the most . . . the most original ideas I've seen in years."

"Thank you." Newton seemed more interested now. "I

thought very few people knew that I was . . . responsible for those things."

Something about the tired, dispassionate way that Newton spoke made him feel slightly ashamed of himself, ashamed of the curiosity that had made him trace down the W. E. Corporation to Farnsworth, and browbeat Farnsworth into arranging this interview. He felt like a child who has tried to gain the attention of an indulgent father and has failed, has instead only disturbed and wearied the man. For a moment he thought that he might be blushing, and was thankful for the dim light in the room in case he were.

"I . . . I've always admired a first-rate mind." He had somehow got caught up in embarrassment and he knew, cursing himself, that he sounded like a schoolboy. But when Newton answered with something modest and polite, Bryce was shocked out of embarrassment by realizing, in an instant, that the other man might well be drunk. He heard the distant, apathetic, slightly blurred speech, saw the distracted, unfocused look in the man's wide eyes, and saw that Newton, almost imperceptibly, was either very drunk—quietly, calmly drunk—or very sick. And he suddenly felt a wave of quick affection—was he drunk himself?—for the thin, lonely man. Was Newton, also, a master of quiet morning drunkenness, looking for—for whatever it was that could supply a sane man in an insane world a reason for not being drunk in the morning? Or was this only one of the notorious aberrations of genius, a kind of wild and lonely abstraction, the ozone of an electrical intelligence?

"Oliver has arranged with you about your salary? And you're satisfied with it?"

"It's all been taken care of very well." He stood up, recognizing that Newton's question closed the interview. "I'm thoroughly content with the salary." And then, before he offered to go, he said, "I wonder if I may ask you a question before I leave, Mr. Newton?"

Newton hardly seemed to hear him; he was still looking out the window, the empty glass held gently in his frail fingers, his face smooth, unlined, yet very old looking. "Certainly, Professor Bryce," he said, his voice very soft, almost a whisper.

He felt embarrassed again, awkward. The man was so impossibly gentle. He cleared his throat, and noticed that, across the room, the parrot was awake, peering at him somewhat curiously as the cats had before. He felt dizzy and was certain now that he was blushing. He stammered, "It really doesn't matter, I guess. I'll . . . I'll ask you some other time."

Newton looked at him as though he had not heard him, but was still waiting to hear. He said, "Certainly. Some other time."

Bryce excused himself, left the room, and walked, squinting, into bright light. When he got downstairs again the cats were gone.

CHAPTER TEN

DURING THE NEXT several months Bryce was busier than he had ever been before in his life. From the moment Brinnarde had led him from the big house and had sent him to the research labs, on the far side of the lake, he had plunged, with a willingness and fervor that were altogether foreign to him, into a multiplicity of jobs that Newton had waiting. There were alloys to be selected and developed, endless tests to be run, unearthly ideal qualifications of heat and acid resistance to be met in plastics, metals, resins and ceramics. This was work for which his training ideally suited him, and he adjusted to it with great rapidity. He had a staff of fourteen beneath him, a huge aluminum shed of a laboratory to work in, a practically limitless budget, a small private house of four rooms and carte blanche—which he never exercised—for plane trips to Louisville, Chicago or New York. There were irritations and confusions of course, especially in having necessary equipment and materials brought in on time, and in occasional petty feuds

among his assistants, but these annoyances were never sufficiently great to hold up the work in more than a few of its
multiple aspects. He was, if not happy, too busy to be unhappy.
He was absorbed, engaged, in a way that he had never been as a
teacher, and he was aware that much in his life was dependent
upon this work. He knew that he had broken completely with
teaching, just as he had broken, years before, with government
work, and that it was imperative that he believe in his present
work. He was too old to fail again, to sink into despair again;
he would never be able to recover. In a series of events that
had begun with a roll of caps and had depended on an absurd,
science fiction speculation, he had fluked into a job that many
men might dream of. He often found himself working far into
the night, absorbed in his work; and he no longer drank in
the mornings. There were deadlines to be met, certain designs
had to be ready for production at certain dates, and he was not
worried about these. He was well ahead of schedule. Occasionally the fact that the work was applied research and not genuinely basic research was a source of some concern to him; but
he was a little too old now, a little too disillusioned, to worry
about points of honor, matters of integrity. Perhaps the only
real moral question was whether or not he was working on a
new weapon, a new means of dismembering men or destroying
cities. And the answer to that was negative. They were building a vehicle to carry instruments around the solar system, and
that in itself was, if not worthwhile, at least harmless.

A routine part of his work consisted of checking his progress
against the portfolio of Newton's specifications that had been
given him by Brinnarde. These papers, which he thought of as
the "master plumber's inventory," consisted largely of specifications for hundreds of minor parts of refrigeration, fuel control

and guidance systems, specifications which called for certain measures of thermal conductivity, electrical resistance, chemical stability, mass, ignition temperature, and the like. It was Bryce's business to find the most thoroughly suitable material, or if none could be found, to find what would be second best. In many cases this was quite easy, so much so that he could not help wondering at Newton's naiveté about materials; but in several cases the specifications could be matched by no known substances. He was forced, in such cases, to talk the thing over with the project engineers and devise the shrewdest possible compromise. The compromise would be delivered, then, to Brinnarde, and would be pronounced upon by Newton. The project engineers told him that they had been having this kind of trouble all along, during the six months the project had been under way; Newton was a genius at design, the overall pattern was the most sophisticated they had ever seen and embodied a thousand startling innovations, but there had been hundreds of compromises already, and the construction of the ship itself was not due to begin for another year. The entire project was scheduled to be finished within six years—by 1990—and everyone seemed to entertain doubts about the probability of finishing by that time. But this speculation did not disturb Bryce very much. Despite the ambiguous nature of his one interview with Newton, he was immensely confident of that strange person's scientific abilities.

Then, on a cool evening three months after he had first come to Kentucky, Bryce made a discovery. It was near midnight and he found himself alone in his private office at one end of the laboratory building, tiredly going over a group of specification sheets, unwilling yet to go home, since the evening was pleasant and he enjoyed the quietness of the lab. He

was idly staring at one of Newton's few sheets of diagrams—
a schematic of the cooling system that was supposed to elimi-
nate re-entry heat—and tracing the relationship of parts, when
some unidentifiable strangeness about the measurements and
computations began vaguely to annoy him. For several minutes he chewed the end of his pencil, staring first at the neatly
laid-out diagrams and then out the window that faced the
lake. There was nothing wrong with the figures, but something
about them disturbed him. He had noticed that before, in the
back of his mind; but it had always been impossible to put
his finger on the discrepancy. Outside, a clear half-moon was
poised over the black lake, and hidden insects clicked remotely.
It all seemed strange—like a lunar landscape. He looked back
to the paper on the desk before him. The central group of figures was a progression of thermal values—values in an irregular sequence—Newton's tentative specifications for a kind of
tubing. Something about the sequence was suggestive; it was
like a logarithmic progression, and yet was not. But then, what
was it? Why should Newton pick this particular set of values,
and not others? It had to be arbitrary. The precise values didn't
count anyway. They were only tentative requirements; it was up
to Bryce to find the actual values for the material that would
come closest to satisfying the specifications. He stared at the
figures on the paper in a kind of gentle hypnosis until the dig-
its seemed to merge and blend before his eyes and to lose all
meaning for him except for their pattern. He blinked and then,
with an effort of will, looked away, staring once again out the
window into the Kentucky night. The moon had changed position, was now obscured by the hills beyond the lake. Across
the black water a faint light burned in the second floor of the
big house, probably in Newton's study, and overhead the stars,

a myriad of faint pinpricks, covered the black sky like specks of luminous powder. Suddenly, with no apparent cause, a bull-frog began to *glunk* outside the window, startling Bryce. The frog continued, unanswered, unchorused, for several minutes, calling with heavy, purposeful vibrancy, crouched wetly some-where; he could visualize its demi-reptilian body huddled, legs beneath chin, in cool, dew-wet grass. The sound seemed for a while to vibrate over the lake, in rhythm, and then it abruptly stopped, leaving Bryce's ears dissatisfied for a moment, waiting for the final beat that never came. But the insects returned, in chorus, and he settled wearily back to the paper before him and it was then that he saw easily, in a brief moment of insight, his eyes merely tracing the familiar figures in an automatic way, what had been bothering him. They were in logarithmic pro-gression; they had to be. But in no familiar logarithm—not to the base ten, or two, or pi—but in some unheard-of one. He picked up his slide rule from the desk and, his weariness gone, began to make trial and error divisions . . .

After an hour he stood up, stretched his arms, and left the office, walking through wet grass to the edge of the lake. The moon was out again; he watched its reflection on the water for a while, and then he stared at Newton's window and said softly aloud the question that had been taking shape in his mind for twenty minutes: "What kind of a man would compute with logarithms to the base twelve?" The light in Newton's window, much fainter than the moon, stared back at him blankly, and at his feet the water washed gently against the shore, in a dim, mindless cadence, monotonous, quiet, and as old as the world.

1988: RUMPLESTILTSKIN

CHAPTER ONE

IN AUTUMN THE mountains around the lake became red and yellow and orange and brown. The water, under a colder sky, was bluer; it reflected in places the colors of the trees on the mountains. When the wind blew, pushing ripples before it, reds and yellows would flash on the water, and leaves would fall.

From the door of his laboratory, Bryce, often lost in thought, would sometimes stare across the water to the mountains, and to the house where T. J. Newton lived. The house was more than a mile distant from the crescent of aluminum and plywood buildings to which the laboratory was joined; at the other side of the crescent, when the sun was shining, the polished hull of the Thing—the Project, the Vehicle, whatever it was—glistened. Sometimes the sight of the silvery monolith would make Bryce feel something resembling pride; sometimes it only seemed ridiculous, like an illustration from a child's book on space; sometimes it frightened him. It was possible for him to stand in his doorway and look directly across the lake to the uninhabited far shore and see the peculiar contrast—which he had observed early and often—between the structures at each end of the panorama: to his right the old Victorian mansion, with bay windows, white clapboarding, huge and useless pillars at its three porches, a home built in heavy-handed and tasteless pride by some unknown and long-dead tobacco or coal or lumber baron more than a century before; and to his left the most austere and futuristic of all constructions, a spaceship. A spaceship standing in a Kentucky pasture, surrounded by autumnal mountains, owned by a man who chose to live in a mansion with one drunken servant, with a French secretary, with parrots, paintings and cats. Between the ship and the house stood the water, the mountains, Bryce himself, and the sky.

One morning in November, when the youthful seriousness of one of his lab assistants had made him feel a twinge of his old despair over scientific work and the airs of young men who practiced it, he went to the doorway and spent several minutes staring at the familiar view. Abruptly, he decided to take a walk; it had never occurred to him before to walk around the lake. There was no reason why he shouldn't.

The air was cold, and for a moment he thought he should return to the lab for his jacket. But the sun was warm, in a mild, November morning way, and by staying along the edge of the water, out of the shade, he was able to keep comfortable enough. He walked in the direction of the big house, away from the construction site and the ship. He was wearing a faded wool plaid shirt, a ten-year-old gift from his dead wife; after a mile of walking he was forced to roll up the sleeves to his elbows, for they had begun prickling with the warmth of his body. His forearms, thin, white and hairy, seemed shock-

ingly pale in the sunlight—the arms of a very old man. Under-
foot was gravel, and occasionally scrub grass. He saw several
squirrels, and a rabbit. Once, out in the lake, a fish jumped.
He passed a few buildings and some kind of metal-working
shop; some men waved at him. One of them spoke to him by
name, but he did not recognize the man. He smiled back, and
waved. He settled to a slow walk, and let his mind wander
aimlessly. Once he stopped and tried to skip a few flat rocks
on the lake and succeeded in forcing one of them to make a
single leap. The others, hitting wrong, all sank the minute they
touched the water. He shook his head at them, feeling foolish.
High overhead a dozen birds flew soundlessly across the sky.
He went on walking.

Before noon he passed the house, which seemed closed and
silent, sitting a few hundred feet back from the water's edge.
He stared for a moment at the upstairs bay window, but could
see nothing save the reflection of the sky on the glass. By the
time the sun was as nearly overhead as it would be at that time
of year, he was walking along the uninhabited shore at the far
edge of the lake. The scrub grass and weeds were thicker now;
there were bushes and goldenrod and a few rotten logs. He
thought momentarily of snakes, which he disliked, but dismissed the thought. He saw a lizard, sitting immobile on a
stone, its eyes like glass. He began to be hungry, and wondered
idly what he would do about it. Tiring, he sat on a log at the
water's edge, loosened his shirt buttons, wiped the back of his
neck with his handkerchief, and stared at the water. He felt
momentarily like Henry Thoreau, and smiled at himself for
the feeling. *Most men lead lives of quiet desperation.* He looked
back toward the house, partly obscured now by trees. Someone,
still quite distant, was walking toward him. He blinked in the

strong light, stared for a few moments, and became gradually aware that it was T. J. Newton. He leaned his elbows on his knees, and waited. He began to feel nervous.

Newton was carrying a small basket on his arm. He was wearing a short-sleeved white shirt and light gray slacks. He walked slowly, his tall body erect, but with a light graceful-ness to the movement. There was an indefinable strangeness about his way of walking, a quality that reminded Bryce of the first homosexual he had ever seen, back when he had been too young to know what a homosexual was. Newton did not walk like that; but then he walked like no one else: light and heavy at the same time.

When Newton was close enough to be heard he said, "I brought some cheese and wine." He was wearing dark glasses.

"Fine." Bryce stood up. "Did you see me when I passed the house?"

"Yes." The log was fairly long and semicircular in shape. Newton sat at the other end of it, placing the basket at his feet. He withdrew a wine bottle and a corkscrew and held them out toward Bryce. "Would you open it?"

"I'll try." He took the bottle, noticing as he did so that Newton's arms were as thin and pale as his own, but hairless. The fingers were very long and slender, with the smallest knuckles he had ever seen. The hands trembled slightly, as Newton handed him the bottle.

The wine was a Beaujolais. Bryce held the bottle, cold and wet, between his knees and began working the corkscrew. This was one operation he was fairly dextrous at, unlike skipping flat rocks on the water. He got the cork out, with a neat and satisfying *pop*, on the first try. Newton walked over with two glasses—not wine glasses, but tumblers—and held them for him while he poured. "Be generous," Newton said, smiling down at him; and he poured the tumblers nearly full. Newton's voice was pleasant; the faint accent seemed quite natural.

The wine was excellent, cool and fragrant in his dry throat. It warmed his stomach instantly with a tinge of the fine old double pleasure of alcohol—physical and spiritual—the pleasure that kept a great many men going, had kept him going for years. The cheese was strong cheddar, old and flaky. They ate and drank silently for several minutes. They were in the shade, and Bryce rolled his sleeves down. Now that he was no longer walking, he was cool again. He wondered why Newton, in his light clothes, did not seem cold. He looked the sort of man who would sit by a fire, wrapped in a shawl—the person whom George Arliss had played in old movies: thin, pale, cold-blooded. But who could say what kind of person he was? He might be a vaguely foreign count in an English comedy, or an aging Hamlet; or the mad scientist, planning discreetly, to blow up the world; or an unostentatious Cortes, quietly building his citadel with local labor. The Cortes notion reminded him of his old idea, never completely forgotten, that Newton might be an extraterrestrial. At this moment almost anything seemed possible; it was not so ridiculous that he, Nathan Bryce, might be drinking wine and eating cheese with a man from Mars. Why not? Cortes had conquered Mexico with about four hundred men; could a single man from Mars do it alone? It seemed possible, as he sat with the wine in his stomach and the sun on his face. Newton sat beside him, chewing delicately, then sipping, his back erect. There was an Ichabod Crane look to him in profile. How could he, Bryce, be sure that if Newton were from Mars he would be the only one from there? Why hadn't he thought of that before? Why not four hundred Martians, or four thousand? He looked at him again, and Newton caught his eye and smiled gravely. From Mars? He was probably a Lithuanian, or from Massachusetts.

Feeling a little drunk—how long had it been since he had been drunk at midday?—he peered inquisitively at Newton and said, "Are you a Lithuanian?"

"No." Newton was looking at the lake and did not turn at Bryce's question. Then he said, abruptly, "This entire lake belongs to me. I bought it."

"That's nice." He finished his glass of wine. It was the last of the bottle.

"A great deal of water," Newton said. Then, turning to him, "How much, do you suppose?"

"How much water?"

"Yes." Newton absently broke off a piece of cheese, and bit into it.

"God. I don't know. Five million gallons? Ten?" He laughed. "I can hardly estimate the amount of sulphuric acid in a beaker." He looked at the lake. "Twenty million gallons? Hell, I don't have to know. I'm a specialist." Then, remembering Newton's reputation, "But you aren't. You know every science that is. Maybe some that aren't."

"Nonsense. I'm only an . . . inventor. If that." He finished his cheese. "I imagine I'm more of a specialist than yourself."

"At what?"

Newton did not answer for a while. Then he said, "That would be hard to say." He smiled again, cryptically. "Do you like straight gin?"

"Not exactly. Maybe."

"I have a bottle in here." Newton reached down to the basket at his feet and took out a bottle. Bryce laughed abruptly.

He could not help it—Ichabod Crane with a fifth of gin in his lunch basket. Newton poured him a generous glassful, and then one for himself. Suddenly he said, still holding the bottle, "I drink too much."

"Everybody drinks too much." Bryce tasted the gin. He did not like it; gin had always tasted like perfume to him. But he drank it. How often does a man have a chance to get drunk with the boss? And how many bosses are Ichabod Crane-Hamlet-Cortes, fresh off the boat from Mars and about to conquer the world by spaceship in the fall of the year? Bryce's back was tired and he let himself slip to the grass and lean against the log, his feet pointing out to the water of the lake. Thirty million gallons? He took another drink of gin and then fished a flattened pack of cigarettes from his pocket and offered one to Newton. Newton was still sitting on the log, and from Bryce's low vantage-point he looked even taller, more distant than ever.

"I smoked once, about a year ago," Newton said. "It made me very sick."

"Oh?" He took a cigarette from the package. "Would you rather I didn't smoke?"

"Yes." Newton looked down at him. "Do you think there'll be a war?"

He held the cigarette speculatively, then flipped it into the lake. It floated. "Aren't there three wars going now? Or four?"

"Three. I mean a war with big weapons. There are nine nations with hydrogen weapons; at least twelve with bacteriological ones. Do you think they'll be used?"

Bryce took a larger sip of gin. "Probably. Sure. I don't know why it hasn't happened yet. I don't know why we haven't drunk ourselves to death yet. Or loved ourselves to death." The Vehicle was across the lake from them, but could not be seen for the trees. Bryce waved his glass in its direction and said, "Is that going to be a weapon? If it is, who needs it?"

"It's not a weapon. Not really." Newton must be drunk. "I won't tell you what it is." And then, "After how long?"

"After how long what?" He felt high, too. Fine. It was a lovely afternoon to be high. It had been a long time.

"Until the big war begins? The one that will ruin everything."

"Why not ruin everything?" He tossed off his drink, reached over to the basket for the bottle. "Everything may need ruining." As he took the bottle he looked up at Newton, but could not see his face because the sun was behind him. "Are you from Mars?"

"No. Would you say ten years? I was taught it would be ten years at least."

"Who teaches things like that?" He poured himself a glassful. "I'd say five years."

"That's not long enough."

"Long enough for what?" The gin did not taste so bad now, even though it was warm in the glass.

"It's not long enough." Newton looked down at him, sadly. "But you're probably wrong."

"All right, three years. Are you from Venus? Jupiter? Philadelphia?"

"No." Then he shrugged. "My name is Rumplestiltskin."

"Rumplestiltskin what?"

Newton reached down, took the bottle from him, poured himself another glass of gin. "Do you think it might not happen at all?"

"Maybe. What would keep it from happening, Rumplestiltskin? Man's higher instincts? Elves live in caves; do you live in a cave, when you're not visiting?"

"Trolls live in caves. Elves live everywhere. Elves have the power of adapting themselves to extraordinarily difficult environments, such as this one." He waved a shaky hand out toward the lake, spilling gin on his shirt. "I am an elf, Doctor Bryce, and I live alone everywhere. Altogether everywhere alone." He stared at the water.

A large group of ducks had settled on the lake about a half-mile from them, probably tired migrants on their way to the Far South. They seemed to float like tiny balloons on the surface of the water, drifting, as if incapable of locomotion. "If you were from Mars, you would be alone, all right," Bryce said, watching the ducks. If he were, he would be like a lone duck on the lake—a tired migrant.

"It's not necessary."

"What isn't necessary?"

"To be from Mars. I imagine you have felt alone often enough, Doctor Bryce. Have felt alienated. Are you from Mars?"

"I don't think so."

"Philadelphia?"

Bryce laughed. "Portsmouth, Ohio. That's farther from here than Mars." With no apparent warning, the ducks on the lake began quacking confusedly. Suddenly they took off in flight, beginning in disarray, but then co-ordinating themselves into something loosely resembling a formation. Bryce watched them disappear over the mountains, still gaining in altitude. He thought fuzzily of the migration of birds, of birds and insects and small furry animals, moving, following old,

old pathways to ancient homes and new deaths. And then the flock of ducks reminded him bitterly of a squadron of missiles he had seen pictured on a magazine cover years before, and this made him think again of the thing he was helping this strange man beside him to build, that sleek, missile-like ship that was supposed to explore or experiment or take pictures or something and that somehow, now, feeling very light and drunk in the mid-afternoon sun, he did not trust, did not trust at all.

Newton stood up, unsteadily, and said, "We can walk to the house. I'll have Brinnarde drive you home from there, if you'd like."

"I'd like." He stood up, brushing leaves from his clothes, and then finished his gin. "I'm too drunk and too old to walk home."

They walked, staggering slightly, in silence. But when they were near the house Newton said, "I hope it will be ten years."

"Why ten years?" Bryce said. "If it's that long the weapons will be even better. They'll blow up everything. The whole business. Maybe even the Lithuanians'll do it. Or the Philadelphians."

Newton looked down at him strangely, and Bryce for a moment felt uneasy. "If we have ten years," Newton said, "it may not happen at all. It may not be able to happen."

"And what's going to stop it then? Human virtue? The Second Coming?" Somehow he could not look Newton in the eye.

For the first time Newton laughed, softly and pleasantly. "Maybe it will be the Second Coming indeed. Maybe it will be Jesus Christ himself. In ten years."

"If he comes," Bryce said, "he'd better watch his step."

"I imagine he'll remember what happened to him the last time," Newton said.

Brinnarde came from the house to meet them. Bryce was relieved: he had begun to feel dizzy in the sunshine.

He had Brinnarde take him directly home, and did not stop by the laboratory. During the drive Brinnarde asked what seemed to be a great many questions, to all of which Bryce gave vague answers. It was five o'clock when he arrived home. He went into the kitchen, which was, as always, a thorough mess. On the wall hung *The Fall of Icarus*, brought from Iowa, and in the sink were his breakfast dishes. He got a cold chicken leg from the refrigerator in the wall, and, chewing on it, staggered tiredly to bed, where he fell quickly asleep, the half-eaten leg beside him on the night-stand. He had a great many dreams, all of them confused, and many of them involving the flight of birds in straggling formation across a cold blue sky . . .

He awoke at four o'clock in the morning, coming wide awake in the darkness with his mouth tasting foul, his head aching and his neck sweating from the heavy woolen collar. His feet felt swollen from walking; he was very thirsty. He sat on the edge of the bed, staring at the luminous dial of the clock for several minutes, and then gingerly he turned on the bedside lamp, closing his eyes before the click. He stood up, blinked his way across the floor to the bathroom, filled the basin with cold water, and drank two glassfuls from his tooth-brush glass while it was filling. He cut off the tap, turned the light on, began unbuttoning the oppressive plaid shirt. In the mirror he saw a patch of his white chest beneath the U of his undershirt, and looked away. He dipped his hands in the water and held them there, letting the coldness stimulate circulation in his wrists. Then he cupped his hands and put water on the back of his neck and on his face. He dried himself hard with a coarse towel, and then brushed his teeth, getting the foul taste from his mouth. He combed his hair, went to the bedroom for a clean shirt—a blue dress shirt this time, but without the frilled front that most men wore.

All the time that he was doing this an old phrase was running through his head: *You pays your money and you takes your choice.*

He fixed himself breakfast in the kitchen, dissolving a coffee pill in hot water and frying himself an omelette, which he doused liberally with sliced mushrooms from a can. He folded the omelette expertly with a spatula, took it out while it was still moist in the center, set it with the coffee on the plastic table, sat, and ate slowly, letting his gin-burdened stomach enclose the squashy thing as gently as he could. It stayed down well enough; and he felt momentarily pleased with himself for not being sick—after having had nothing since yesterday's breakfast but wine, cheese and straight gin. He shuddered. He could at least have eaten a few of those PA pills that people ate when they didn't want the trouble of an honest dinner. PA was protein algae—a nasty thought, eating pond scum instead of liver and onions. But maybe he should use them, considering the population and the Asian dust-bowls that had put the Fascists back in in China—and thus in the "free world" of dictators, demagogues and hedonists once more—and was making liver and onions or beef and potatoes harder and harder to find. We'll all be eating pond scum and fish oil and Erlenmeyer flask carbohydrate in another twenty years, he thought, finishing the omelette. When there's no more room for the chickens they'll keep the eggs in museums. Maybe the Smithsonian will have a preserved omelette, in plastic. He drank his coffee, itself partly synthetic, and thought of the old biologists' maxim that a chicken is an egg's way of reproducing itself. This made him think, grimly, that some hot-shot young biologist with a crew cut and frilly trousers would probably find a way more efficient than the egg's natural one, eliminating the chicken altogether. But, then, it wouldn't be a young hot-shot; T. J. Newton would be the man more likely to come out with a navel egg—like a navel orange—all wrapped in gay plastic and marketed by World Enterprises Corporation. A self-reproducing egg: you plant it in pond water and it grows like a plastic bead necklace, popping forth a new egg daily. But it would not cackle with satisfaction afterward, nor could it ever produce a gorgeously prideful bantam rooster, a game-cock, or a stupid hen for a child to chase. Or a fried chicken dinner.

Then, finishing the coffee, he looked up and saw *The Fall of Icarus* and, knowing now what the picture was coming to mean to him, he set the cup down and said aloud, "Quit playing intellectual games, Bryce." You pays your money and you takes your choice: Mars or Massachusetts? And, still looking at the leg and arm of the sky-fallen boy in the ocean in the serene picture on the wall, he thought, *Friend or foe?* He kept staring at the picture. *Destroyer or preserver?* Newton's words were in his head. "It may be the Second Coming indeed." But Icarus had failed, had burned and drowned, while Daedalus, who had not gone so high, had escaped from his lonely island. Not to save the world, however. Maybe even to destroy it, for he had invented flights; and destruction, when it came, would come from the air. Brightness falls from the air, he thought; I grow sick; I must die; Lord have mercy on us. He shook his head, trying to keep his mind from wandering. The problem now was Mars or Massachusetts; everything else was secondary. And what did he know now? There was Newton's accent, his appearance, his way of walking. There were the productions of his mind, implying a technology more alien than the Ptol-emaic system of astronomy. There were those fantastic loga-rithms, there was his being slightly totty the two times Bryce had seen him, which could imply the ungodly loneliness that an extraterrestrial might feel, or an inability to withstand the bruises of the culture he had fallen into. But being totty was so damnably human, and that canceled out the other argu-ment. Wouldn't it be unlikely that an extraterrestrial would be affected by alcohol as a man is? But Newton must be a man—or something like a man. He would have a man's blood chemistry; he should be able to get drunk. But that would still be more plausible if he were from Massachusetts. Or Lithu-ania. But why not a drunken Martian? Christ himself drank wine, and he came down from heaven—a wine-bibber, the Pharisees said. A wine-bibber from outer space. Why did his mind keep wandering from the point? Cortes had been given tequila, probably; and he was another Second Comer: the blue-eyed god, Quetzalcoatl, come to save the peons from the Aztecs. In ten years? Logarithms to the base twelve. And what else? *And what else?*

CHAPTER TWO

SOMETIMES HE FELT as if he must be going insane in the way that humans did; and yet it was theoretically impossible that an Anthean could be insane. He did not understand what was happening to him, or what had happened. They had prepared him for the extraordinary difficulty of his work, and he had been selected for it because of his physical strength and his ability to adapt. He had known from the outset that there were many ways in which he might fail, that the entire thing was an enormous risk, an extravagant plan by a people who could find nowhere else to turn; and he was prepared for failure. But he had not been prepared for what had, in fact, happened. The plan itself was going so well—the great amounts of money made, the construction of the ship begun with almost no difficulty, the failure of anyone (although, he believed, many had suspected and were suspecting) to recognize him for what he was—and the possibility of success was now so close. And he, the Anthean, a superior being from a superior race, was losing control, becoming a degenerate, a drunkard, a lost and foolish creature, a renegade and, possibly, a traitor to his own.

Sometimes he blamed Betty Jo for it, for his own weakness in the face of this world. How human he had become, to rationalize that way! He blamed her for his going native and becoming obsessed with vague guilts and vaguer doubts. She had taught him to drink gin; and she had shown him an aspect of strong and comfortable and hedonistic and unthinking humanity that his fifteen years of studying television had left him unaware of. She had shown him a drowsy, drunken vitality that Antheans might never, in their god-awful timelessness and wisdom, have known of or dreamed of. He felt like a man who has been surrounded by reasonably amiable, silly, and fairly intelligent animals, and has gradually discovered that their concepts and relationships are more complex than his training could have led him to suspect. Such a man might discover that, in one or more of the many aspects of weighing and judging that are available to a high intelligence, the animals who surround him and who foul their own lairs and eat their own filth might be happier and wiser than he.

Or was it merely that a man surrounded by animals long enough became more of an animal than he should? But the analogy was unfair, was not right. He shared with the humans an ancestry that was closer than the common kinship in the family of mammals and furry creatures in general. Both he and the humans were articulate, fairly rational creatures, capable of insight, prediction, and emotions loosely named love, pity, and reverence. And, he had found, capable of drunkenness.

Antheans had some familiarity with alcohol, although sugars and fats played a very minor part in the ecology of that world. There was a sweet berry from which a kind of light wine was sometimes made; pure alcohol could, of course, be synthesized easily enough, and very occasionally an Anthean might become drunk. But steady drinking did not exist; there was no such thing as an alcoholic Anthean. He had never in his life heard of anyone on Anthea drinking as he, on Earth, drank—daily now, and steadily.

He did not become drunk in quite the same way that the humans did; or at least he thought he did not. He never wished to become unconscious, or riotously happy, or godlike; he only wanted relief, and he was not certain from what. He did not have hangovers, no matter how much he drank. He was alone most of the time. It might have been difficult for him not to drink.

After he left Bryce to be driven home by Brinnarde, he walked into the never used living room of his house and stood silently for a minute, enjoying the coolness of the room and its quiet dimness. One of the cats got up lazily from a couch, stretched itself, came over to him, and began rubbing itself against his leg, purring. He looked at it fondly; he had grown to like cats very much. They had a quality that reminded him of Anthea, even though there was no animal resembling them there. But they hardly seemed to belong to this world either.

Betty Jo came in from the kitchen, wearing an apron. She looked at him silently for a moment, her eyes gentle, and then she said, "Tommy?"

"Yes?"

"Tommy, Mr. Farnsworth called you from New York. Twice." He shrugged. "He calls almost every day now, doesn't he?"

"Yes he does, Tommy." She smiled softly. "Anyhow he said it was important and you should call him back right away."

He knew well enough that Farnsworth was having problems, but they would have to wait for a while. He did not feel up to dealing with them just yet. He looked at his watch. Almost five o'clock. "Tell Brinnarde to put a call through at eight," he said. "If Oliver calls again tell him I'm busy and that I'll talk to him at eight."

"All right." She hesitated a moment and then said, "Do you want me to come sit with you? And talk maybe?"

He saw the look on her face, the hopeful look that he knew meant she was as dependent upon him as he was on her for companionship. What strange companions they had become! Yet, though he knew her to be as lonely as himself and to share his sense of alienation, he felt unable even now to grant her the right to sit with him in silence. He smiled as pleasantly as he could. "I'm sorry, Betty Jo. I have to be alone for a while." How difficult that practiced smile was becoming for him!

"Sure, Tommy," she said. She turned, too quickly. "I have to get back to the kitchen." At the door she turned back to him. "You let me know when you want supper, hear? I'll bring it up."

"Fine." He walked to the staircase and decided to ride the little escalator chair, which he had not used for weeks. He was beginning to feel very tired. As he sat down, one of the cats sprang into his lap, and with an unaccustomed shudder, he flung it off. It hit the floor soundlessly, shook itself, and walked off unperturbed, not deigning to look back at him. He thought, looking at the cat, if only you were the intelligent species on this world. And then, smiling wryly, maybe you are.

One time, more than a year before, he had mentioned to Farnsworth that he was becoming interested in music. This had been only partly true, since the melodies and tonal system of human music had always been mildly unpleasant to him. He had, however, become interested in music historically, since he had an historian's interest in almost all aspects of human folklore and art—an interest built up by the years of studying television, and continued through long nights of reading, here on Earth. Farnsworth, shortly after that casual mention of the fact, had presented him with a brilliantly accurate, octaphonic speaker system—several components of which were based on W. E. Corporation patents—and the necessary amplifiers, sound sources, and the like. Three men with MS degrees in electrical engineering had built the components into the study for him. It was a bother, but he had not wanted to hurt Farnsworth's feelings. They had arranged all of the controls on one brass panel—he would have preferred something less scientific than flat brass—perhaps delicately painted china or porcelain—at one end of a bookcase. Farnsworth had also given him an automatic magazine of five hundred recordings, all done on the little steel balls that W. E. Corp. held the patents on and with which the corporation had earned at least twenty million dollars. You pressed a button, and a ball the size of a pea fell into place in the cartridge. Its molecular structure was then followed by a tiny, slow-moving scanner, and the patterns were converted into the sounds of orchestras or bands or guitarists or voices. Newton almost never played music. He had tried some symphonies and quartets on Farnsworth's insistence, but they meant almost nothing to him. It was odd that their meaning was so obscure to him. Some of the other arts, although misinterpreted and patronized by Sunday television (the most dull and pretentious television of all), had been able to move him greatly—especially sculpture and painting.

Perhaps he saw as the humans saw, but could not hear as they heard.

When he came to his room, musing about cats and men, he decided, on an impulse, to play some music. He pressed the button for a Haydn symphony that Farnsworth had told him he should hear. After a moment the sounds came on, militant and precise and, to him, of no logical or aesthetic consequence. He was like an American listening to Chinese music. He fixed himself a drink from a gin bottle on the shelf and drank it straight, trying to follow the sounds. He was preparing to seat himself on the sofa when there came a sudden knocking on the door. Startled, he dropped his glass. It broke at his feet. For the first time in his life he shouted, "What in hell is it?" *How human had he become?*

Betty Jo's voice, sounding frightened, said from behind the door, "It's Mr. Farnsworth again, Tommy. He insisted. He said I had to get you ..."

His voice was softer now, but still angry. "Tell him no. Tell him I'm not seeing anyone before tomorrow; I'm not talking to anyone."

For a minute there was silence. He stared at the broken glass at his feet, then kicked the larger pieces under the couch. Then Betty Jo's voice: "All right, Tommy. I'll tell him." She paused. "You rest now, Tommy. Hear?"

"All right," he said, "I'll rest."

He heard her footsteps receding from the door. He went to the bookcase. There was no other glass. He started to shout for Betty Jo, instead picked up the nearly-full bottle, twisted the cap off, and began to drink from it. He switched off the Haydn—who could expect him to understand music like that?—and then switched on a collection of folk music, old

Negro songs, Gullah music. There was, at least, something in the words of those songs that he could understand.

A rich and weary voice came from the speakers:

> "Every time I go Miss Lulu house
> Old dog done bite me
> Every time I go Miss Sally house
> Bulldog done bite me . . ."

He smiled thoughtfully; the words of the song seemed to reach something in him. He settled himself on the couch with the bottle. He began to think about Nathan Bryce and about the conversation they had had together that afternoon.

He had imagined from their first meeting that Bryce suspected him: the very fact that the chemist had insisted on the interview was itself a kind of giveaway. He had made himself certain, through expensive investigation, that Bryce represented no one other than himself—that he did not work for the FBI, as did at least two of the construction workers at the missile site, nor for any other government agency. But then, if Bryce had somehow come to suspect him and his purposes—as, certainly, Farnsworth and probably several others had—why had he, Newton, gone out of his way to cultivate an afternoon's intimacy with the man? And why had he been dropping hints about himself, talking about the war and the Second Coming, calling himself Rumplestiltskin—that evil little dwarf who came from nowhere to weave straw into gold and to save the princess's life with his unheard-of knowledge, the stranger whose final purpose was to steal the princess's child? The only way to defeat Rumplestiltskin was to uncover his identity, to name him.

"Sometime I feel like a motherless child;
Sometime I feel like a motherless child;
Glory, Hallelujah!"

And why, he thought abruptly, had Rumplestiltskin given the princess a chance to escape the bargain? Why had he given her that three-day respite in which to discover his name? Was it simply over-confidence—for who would ever imagine or guess at a name like that one?—or did he want to be found out, caught, deprived of the object of his deceit and magic? And for himself, Thomas Jerome Newton, whose magic and whose deceptions were greater than those of any enchanter or elf in any fairy-tale—and he had read them all—did he now want to be found out, caught?

"This man he come round to my door
He say he don't like me
He come; he standing at my door
He say he don't like me."

Why, thought Newton, his bottle in his hand, would I want to be found out? He stared at the label on the bottle, feeling very strange, dizzy. Abruptly, the recording ended. There was a pause, while another ball rolled into place. He took a long, shocking drink. Then, from the speakers, an orchestra boomed, assaulting his ears.

He stood up wearily, and blinked. He felt very weak—it seemed as if he had not been so weak since that day, now so many years ago, when, frightened and alone, he had been sick in a barren field, in November. He walked to the panel, turned off the music. Then he walked to the television controls and turned them on—maybe a Western . . .

The large picture of the heron on the far wall began to fade. When it was gone it was replaced by the head of a handsome man with the falsely serious stare in his eyes that is cultivated by politicians, faith healers, and evangelists. The lips moved soundlessly, while the eyes stared.

Newton turned up the volume. The head gained a voice, saying, ". . . of the United States as a free and independent nation, we must gird up our loins like men, with the free world behind us, and face the challenges, the hopes and fears of the world. We must remember that the United States, regardless of what the uninformed may say, is *not* a second-rate power. We must remember that freedom will conquer, we must . . ."

Suddenly Newton realized that the man speaking was the President of the United States, and he was speaking the bombast of the hopeless. He turned a switch. A bedroom scene appeared on the screen. Some tired suggestive jokes were made by the man and woman, both of them in pajamas. He turned the switch again, hoping for a Western. He liked Westerns. But what appeared on the screen was a propaganda piece, paid for by the government, about the American virtues and strengths. There were pictures of white New England churches, field hands—always one smiling Negro in each group—and maple trees. These films seemed more and more common lately; and, like so many popular magazines, more and more wildly chauvinistic—more committed than ever to the fantastic lie that America was a nation of God-fearing small towns, efficient cities, healthy farmers, kindly doctors, bemused housewives, philanthropic millionaires.

"My God," he said aloud. "My God, you frightened, self-pitying hedonists. Liars! Chauvinists! Fools!"

He turned the switch again and a night club scene appeared on the screen, with soft music as background. He let it stay, watching the movement of bodies on the dance floor, the men and women dressed like peacocks, embracing one another while the music played.

And what am I, he thought, if not a frightened, self-pitying hedonist? He finished the bottle of gin, and then looked at his hands holding the bottle, staring now at the artificial fingernails, shining like translucent coins in the flickering light from the television screen. He looked at them for several minutes, as though he were seeing them for the first time.

Then he stood up and walked shakily to a closet. From a shelf he took a box that was about the size of a shoebox. On the inside of the closet door hung a full-length mirror. He looked at himself, at his tall, skinny frame, for a moment. Then he went back to the couch and set the box on the marble-topped coffee table in front of him. From it he took a small plastic bottle. On the table sat an empty bowl-shaped ashtray, of Chinese porcelain; Farnsworth had given it to him. He poured the liquid from the bottle into the ashtray, set the bottle down, and then dipped the fingertips of both his hands into the tray, as if it were a finger bowl. He held them there for a minute, and then took them out and slapped his hands together, hard. The fingernails fell on to the marble table with small, tinkling sounds. The fingers were smooth at the ends now, the tips flexible but somewhat sore.

From the television came the sound of jazz, with a loud, insistent rhythm.

He stood up, walked to the door of the room, locked it. Then he went back to the box on the table, and took from it a ball of something resembling cotton, and dipped the ball into the liquid for a moment. His hands, he noticed, were trembling. He knew, too, that he was drunker than he had ever been. But that, apparently, was not drunk enough.

Then he went to the mirror and held the damp ball against each of his ears until the synthetic earlobes fell off. Unbuttoning his shirt, he removed false nipples and hair from his chest in the same manner. The hair and nipples were attached to a thin, porous sheet, and they came off together. He took these things and laid them on the coffee table. Walking back to the mirror he began speaking in his own language, first softly and then loudly, to drown out the jazz from the television set, quoting a poem that he himself had written in his youth. The sounds did not come well from his tongue. He was too drunk; or he was losing the ability to speak in the Anthean sibilants. Then, breathing heavily, he took a small, tweezer-like instrument from the box and stood in front of the mirror and carefully removed the thin, colored plastic membrane from each of his eyes. Still struggling to speak his poem, he blinked at himself with the eyes whose irises opened vertically, like a cat's.

He stared at himself a long time, and then he began to cry. He did not sob, but tears came from his eyes—tears exactly like a human's tears—and slid down his narrow cheeks. He was crying in despair.

Then he spoke aloud, to himself, in English. "Who are you?" he said. "And where do you belong?"

His own body stared back at him; but he could not recognize it as his own. It was alien, and frightening.

He got himself another bottle. The music had stopped. An announcer was saying, ". . . ballroom of the Seelbach Hotel in downtown Louisville, brought to you live by Worldcolor— films and developers for all that's best in photography . . ."

Newton did not look at the screen; he was opening the bottle. A woman's voice began to speak: "To store up memories of the holidays ahead, of the children, the traditional family feast at Thanksgiving and Christmas, there is nothing more lovely than Worldcolor prints, filled with glowing life . . ."

And on the couch, Thomas Jerome Newton now lay drinking, his gin bottle open, his nailless fingers trembling, his cat-like eyes glazed and staring at the ceiling in anguish . . .

CHAPTER THREE

ON A SUNDAY morning five days after his drunken conversation with Newton, Bryce was at home, trying to read a detective novel. He was seated by the electric heater in his small, pre-fabricated living-room, was dressed only in his green flannelette pajamas, and was drinking his third cup of black coffee. He felt better this morning than he had lately; his concern with Newton's identity did not plague him so much as it had for the past several days. The question was still the paramount one in his mind; but he had decided on a sort of policy—if watchful waiting could be called a policy—and had managed to dismiss the problem, if not from his thoughts, at least from his continual scrutiny. The detective novel was pleasantly dull enough; the weather outside had turned bitterly cold. He was comfortable by his would-be fireplace, and he felt no sense of urgency about anything. On the wall to his left hung *The Fall of Icarus*. He had moved it there from the kitchen two days before.

He was about half-way through the book when a faint knock came at his front door. He got up with some irritation, wondering who in hell would call on him on a Sunday morning. There was social life enough among the staff; but he rigorously avoided it, and he had few friends. He had no friend close enough to come calling on a Sunday morning before lunch. He got his bathrobe from the bedroom and then opened the front door.

Outside in the gray morning, shivering in a light nylon jacket, was Newton's housekeeper.

She smiled at him and said, "Doctor Bryce?"

"Yes?" He could not remember her name, although Newton had mentioned it in his presence once. There were a good many rumors about Newton and this woman. "Come in and get warm," he said.

"Thanks." She came in quickly, but apologetically, closing the door behind her. "Mr. Newton sent me."

"Oh?" He led her to the electric fire. "You need a heavier coat."

She seemed to blush—or perhaps it was only the redness of her cheeks from the cold. "I don't get out much."

After he had helped her off with her jacket, she bent over the heater and began warming her hands. Bryce seated himself and watched her thoughtfully, waiting for her to bring up the reason for her call. She was not an unattractive woman—full-mouthed, black-haired, heavy-bodied beneath her plain blue dress. She must be about his own age, and like himself she dressed in old-fashioned clothes. She wore no makeup, but, with the reddening of her complexion from the cold, she did not need any. Her breasts were heavy, like those of peasant women in Russian propaganda films; and she would have had the perfect, monumental "earth mother" look if it had not been for her shy, self-effacing eyes and her hill-billy manner and voice. Beneath the half-sleeves of her dress there was a light growth of black hair on her arms, soft and pleasant looking. He liked that, as he liked the way that she did not pluck her eyebrows.

Abruptly she straightened up, smiled at him more comfortably now, and spoke. "It isn't like a wood fire."

For a moment he didn't understand what she meant. Then, nodding at the red-glowing heater, he said, "No, it certainly isn't." And then, "Why don't you sit down?"

She took the chair across from him, leaned back, and put her feet up on the ottoman. "Doesn't smell like a wood fire either." She looked thoughtful. "I lived on a farm and I can still remember wood fires in the morning when I was hopping around trying to get dressed. I'd lay my clothes on the hearth to warm them up and I'd stand and keep my backside warm by the fire. I can remember how the fire smelled. But I haven't smelled a wood fire in—God knows—twenty years."

"I haven't either," he said.

"Nothing smells as good as it used to," she said. "Not even coffee, the way they make it. Most things don't smell at all any more."

"Do you want a cup? Of coffee?"

"Sure," she said. "You want me to get it?"

"I'll get it," he stood up, finishing off his cup. "I was ready for another one anyway."

He went to the kitchen and fixed two cups, using the coffee pills that were practically all you could buy these days, ever since the country had broken relations with Brazil. He brought them in on a tray, and she smiled up at him pleasantly as she took hers. She looked very comfortable, like an old, good-tempered dog—with neither pride nor philosophy to hinder its comfort.

He sat down, sipping. "You're right," he said, "nothing much smells as it used to. Or maybe we're too old to remember exactly."

She continued smiling. Then she said, "He wants to know if you'll go to Chicago with him. Next month."

"Mr. Newton?"

"Um hmm. There's a meeting. He said you'd probably know about it."

"A meeting?" He drank his coffee speculatively for a moment. "Oh. The Institute of Chemical Engineers. Why does he want to go to that?"

"Don't know," she said. "He told me if you wanted to go with him he'd come by this afternoon and talk about it. You won't be working?"

"No," he said. "No. I don't work on Sundays." He had not changed his casual tone of voice, but his mind was beginning to race. There was an opportunity here, being dropped in his lap. There was a plan he had half formed two days before; and if Newton were definitely coming by the house . . . "I'll be glad to talk to him about it." And then, "Did he say when he would come?"

"No, he didn't." She finished her coffee, set the cup on the floor beside her chair. She certainly makes herself at home, he thought, but he did not mind the way that she did it. It was genuine informality, and not the affected kind that men like Professor Canutti, and all his crew-cut peers back at Iowa, practiced.

"He hasn't been saying much lately at all." There was a hint of strain in her voice when she said this. "In fact I hardly ever see him any more." There was something grim in her voice, too, and Bryce wondered what there could possibly be between these two. And then it occurred to him that her being here was an opportunity, too—one that he might never have again.

"Has he been sick?" *If he could start her talking . . .*

"Not that I know of. He's funny. He takes moods." She was staring at the glowing heat element in front of her, not looking at him. "Sometimes he talks to that Frenchman, Brinnarde his name is, and other times he talks to me. Sometimes he just sits in his room. For days. Or he'll drink; but you can hardly tell it."

"What does Brinnarde do? What's his job?"

"I don't know." She looked at him fleetingly and then back to the fire. "I think he's a body-guard." She turned again to him, her face worried, anxious. "You know, Mister Bryce, he carries a gun with him. And you watch the way he moves. He's quick." She shook her head, as a mother might. "I don't trust him and I don't think Mr. Newton should either."

"A lot of wealthy men have body-guards. Besides, Brinnarde's a kind of secretary too, isn't he?"

She laughed, a short, wry laugh. "Mr. Newton don't write letters."

"No. I suppose not."

Then, still staring at the heater, she said, meekly, "Could I have a little drink, please?"

"Sure." He stood up almost too quickly. "Gin?"

She looked up at him. "Yes please, gin." There was something plaintive about her and Bryce realized, abruptly, that she must be very lonely, must have practically no one to talk to. He felt pity for her—a lost, anachronistic hill-billy—and at the same time excitement at the realization that she was dead ripe to be pumped for information. He could oil her up with a little gin, let her stare at the fire for awhile, and wait for her to talk. He smiled at himself, feeling Machiavellian.

When he was in the kitchen, getting the gin bottle down from the shelf over the sink, she said, from the living-room, "Would you put some sugar in it, please?"

"Sugar?" That was pretty far out.

"Yes. About three spoons."

"Okay," he said, shaking his head. And then, "I've forgotten your name."

Her voice was still strained—as if she were trying to keep from trembling, or from crying. "My name's Betty Jo, Mr. Bryce. Betty Jo Mosher."

There was a kind of soft dignity about the way she answered him that made him feel ashamed for not having remembered her name. He put sugar in a glass, began filling it with gin, and felt further ashamed for what he was about to do—for using her. "Are you from Kentucky?" he said, as politely as he could. He filled the glass almost full, and stirred it.

"Yes. I'm from Irvine. About seven miles out of Irvine. That's north of here."

He carried it in to her and she took it gratefully, but with an attempt at reserve that was both touching and ridiculous. He was beginning to like this woman. "Are your parents living?" He remembered that he was supposed to be pumping her about Newton, not herself. Why did his mind always wander from the point, the real point?

"Mother's dead." She took a sip of the gin, rolled it around in her mouth speculatively, swallowed it, blinked. "I sure like gin," she said. "Daddy sold the farm to the government for a . . . a hydro . . ."

"Hydroponics station?"

"That's right. Where they make that nasty food out of tanks. Anyway, daddy's on relief now—up in Chicago in a development—just like I was, in Louisville, until I met Tommy."

"Tommy?"

She smiled wryly. "Mr. Newton. I call him Tommy sometimes. I used to think he liked it."

He took a breath, looking away from her, and said, "When did you meet him?"

She took another drink of her gin, savored it, swallowed. Then she laughed softly. "In an elevator. I was going up in this elevator in Louisville, to get my country welfare check, and Tommy was in it. Lord, was he peculiar looking! I could see right off. And then he broke his leg in the elevator."

"Broke his leg?"

"That's right. Sounds funny as hell, but that's what he did. The elevator must've been too much for him. If you knew how light he was . . ."

"How light?"

"Lord yes, he's light. You could pick him up with one hand. His bones must have no more strength than a bird's. I tell you he's a peculiar man. Lord, he's a nice man; and he's so smart and rich, and so patient. But, Mr. Bryce . . ."

"Yes?"

"Mr. Bryce, I think he's sick, I think he's sick bad. I think he's sick in his body—My God, you ought to see the pills he takes!—and I think he has . . . troubles in his mind. I want to help, but I never know where to begin. And he wouldn't ever let a doctor come near him." She finished her glass of gin, and leaned forward, as if to gossip. But there was grief on her face—grief too genuine to be faked as an excuse for gossip. "Mr. Bryce, I don't think he ever sleeps. I been with him now for almost a year, and I've never seen him asleep. He's just not human."

Bryce's mind was opening like a lens. A chill was spreading from the nape of his neck, across his shoulders, down his backbone.

"Do you want more gin?" he asked. And then, feeling something that was half laugh, half sob, he said, "I'll join you . . ."

She had two more drinks before she left. She did not tell him very much more about Mr. Newton—probably because he did not want to ask her any more, did not feel as though he had to. But when she left—not staggering at all, for she could hold her liquor like a sailor—she said, as she put on her coat, "Mr. Bryce, I'm a silly, ignorant woman, but I really appreciated talking to you."

"It was a pleasure for me," he said. "Feel free to come back whenever you like."

She blinked at him. "Can I?"

He hadn't meant it literally, but he said now, and meant it, "I want you to come back." And then, "I don't have many people to talk to, either."

"Thank you," she said, and then, as she went out into the winter noon, "That makes three of us, doesn't it . . . ?"

He did not know how many hours he would have before Newton arrived; but he knew he would have to act quickly if he were going to be ready in time. He felt terribly excited and nervous, and while he was dressing he kept muttering, "It can't be Massachusetts, it has to be Mars. It has to be Mars . . ." Did he want it to be Mars?

When he was dressed he put on his overcoat and left the house for the laboratory—a five-minute walk. It was snowing outside now, and the coldness took his attention, for a moment, off the ideas whirling in his mind, the riddle that he was about to solve once and for all, if he could set up the apparatus properly, and set it up in time.

Three of his assistants were in the lab, and he spoke to them gruffly, refusing to answer their comments on the weather. He could feel their curiosity when he began dismantling the small apparatus in the metals lab—the device they used for X-ray stress and analysis—but he pretended not to notice the raised eyebrows. It did not take long: he merely had to remove the bolts that held the camera and the light-weight cathode ray generator to their frames. He was able to carry them easily enough by himself. He made certain the camera was loaded— loaded with W. E. Corp. high-speed X-ray film—and then he left, carrying the camera in one hand, the cathode ray outfit in the other. Before closing the door he said to the other men, "Look, why don't you three take the afternoon off? Okay?"

They looked a bit dazed, but one of them said, "Okay, sure, Doctor Bryce," and looked at the others.

"Fine." He shut the door and left.

Next to the imitation fireplace in Bryce's living-room was an air-conditioning vent, now unused. After twenty minutes of work, and some swearing, he managed to install the camera behind its grille-work, with the shutter wide open. Fortunately the W. E. film was, like so many of Newton's patents, a vast technical improvement over its predecessors; it was totally unaffected by visible light. Only the X-rays could expose it.

The tube in the generator was also a W. E. Corp. device; it worked like a strobe light, giving one instant, concentrated flash of X-rays—extremely useful for high-speed vibration studies. It was even more useful, perhaps, for what Bryce now had in mind. He installed it in the bread drawer in his kitchen, aiming it, through the wall, toward the open-lensed camera. Then he brought the electric cord from the front of the drawer and plugged it into the appliance socket over the sink. He left the drawer partly open so that he could reach his hand in and flip the switch on the side of the little transformer that supplied power to the tube.

He went back into the living-room and carefully placed his most comfortable chair directly between the camera and the cathode ray tube. Then he sat down, in another chair, to wait for Thomas Jerome Newton.

CHAPTER FOUR

THE WAIT WAS a long one. Bryce became hungry; he tried to eat a sandwich, but could not finish it. He paced the floor, picked up his detective novel again, could not concentrate on the reading. Every few minutes he would go into the kitchen and check the position of the cathode ray tube in the bread drawer. Once, deciding on impulse to make certain the instrument was working properly, he flicked the switch to "on," waited for it to heat up, and then pressed the button that made the invisible flash—the flash that would go through the wall, through the chair, through the camera lens, and expose the film in its holder at the back of the camera. And, right after pressing the button, he cursed himself silently and viciously: by fooling around stupidly, he had exposed the film.

It took him twenty minutes to remove the grate from the air-duct again and to get the camera out. Then he had to remove the film—it had the brownish color now that meant it had been exposed properly—and replaced it with another sheet from the camera's magazine. Then, in a sweat for fear that Newton might knock on the door at any moment, he reinstalled the camera in the duct, checked the lens, shakily but carefully pointed the camera toward the chair, and replaced the grill. He made sure the lens was lined up with a hole in the grille-work, so that no metal would interfere.

He had his sleeves rolled up and was washing his hands when the knock came at the front door. He forced himself to walk slowly to it, still carrying a towel in his hands, and opened the door.

Standing in the snow was T. J. Newton, wearing sunglasses and a light jacket. He was smiling slightly, almost ironically it seemed, and, unlike Betty Jo, he did not appear to be at all cold. Mars, Bryce thought, letting him in, Mars is a cold planet.

"Good afternoon," Newton said. "I hope I'm not interrupting you."

Bryce tried to keep his voice steady, and was surprised at himself for being able to do so. "Not at all. I wasn't doing anything. Won't you sit down?" He made a gesture toward the chair by the air-duct. He thought, as he did this, of Damocles, of the throne beneath the sword.

"No," Newton said. "No, thank you. I've been sitting all morning." He removed his jacket and placed it on the back of the chair. He was wearing, as always, a short-sleeved shirt. The way the sleeves stood out at the sides made his arms look like pipestems.

"Let me fix you a drink." If he had a drink he might sit down.

"No thank you. I'm . . . on the wagon right now." Newton walked over to the side wall and examined Bryce's picture. He stood for a moment, silently, while Bryce seated himself. Then he said, "A fine painting, Doctor Bryce. It's a Brueghel, isn't it?"

"Yes." Of course it was a Brueghel. Anybody would know it was a Brueghel. Why didn't Newton sit down? Bryce began cracking his knuckles, and then stopped. Newton absently brushed some drops of melted snow from his hair. Had he been any taller the gesture would have scraped his knuckles on the ceiling.

"What is it called?" Newton said. "The painting."

Newton should know that: the picture was famous enough. "It's called *The Fall of Icarus*. That's Icarus in the water."

Newton continued looking at it. "It's very fine," he said. "And the landscape is much like ours is. The mountains, snow, and the water." He turned, looking now at Bryce. "But of course, in the picture, someone is plowing a field and the sun is lower. It must be later in the day . . ."

Annoyed, still nervous, Bryce's voice was snappish. "Why not earlier?" he said.

Newton's smile was very strange. His eyes seemed focused on something distant. "It couldn't very well have been in the morning, could it?"

Bryce did not answer. But Newton was right, of course. The sun was at noon when Icarus fell. He must have fallen a long way. In the picture, the sun was half-way below the horizon, and Icarus, leg and knee flailing above the water— the water in which he was about to drown, unnoticed, for his foolhardiness—was shown at the moment after impact. He must have been falling since noon.

Newton interrupted this speculation. "Betty Jo told me that you're willing to go to Chicago with me."

"Yes. But tell me, why are you going to Chicago?"

Newton made a gesture that seemed very strange for him—he shrugged his shoulders and held his palms outward. He must have picked that up from Brinnarde. Then he said, "Oh, I need more chemists. I thought it would be a good way to hire them."

"And me?"

"You're a chemist. Or a chemical engineer, rather."

Bryce hesitated before he spoke. What he was going to say would be rude, but Newton seemed not to mind candor. "You have a lot of personnel men, Mr. Newton," he said. Then he forced a laugh. "I had to fight my way through an army of them before I was able to meet you."

"Yes," Newton said. He turned and glanced again at the picture momentarily, and then he said, "Perhaps what I really want is a . . . vacation. A visit to a new place."

"You've never been to Chicago before?"

"No, I'm afraid I'm something of a recluse in this world."

Bryce almost blushed at the remark. He turned toward the artificial fire and said, "Chicago at Christmas time is not the best place in the world for a vacation."

"I don't really object to the cold weather," Newton said. "Do you?"

Bryce laughed nervously. "I'm not as immune to it as you seem to be. But I can stand it."

"Good." He went over to the chair, picked up his jacket and began putting it on. "I'm glad you'll be going with me."

Seeing the other man—or was he a man?—preparing to leave, Bryce became panicky. He might never have another chance. "Just a minute," he said lamely, "I'm going to . . . to fix myself a drink."

Newton said nothing. Bryce left the room and walked into the kitchen. Going through the door he turned to see if Newton might still be standing behind the chair. His heart sank: Newton had walked back over to the picture, was standing in front of it again, gazing gravely. He was half bent over, since his head was at least a foot higher than the picture itself.

Bryce poured himself a double Scotch and filled the glass with tap water. He did not like ice in his drinks. He tossed off a swallow of it, standing by the sink, silently cursing the bad luck that had made Newton decide to stand.

Then, when he walked back into the living room, he saw that Newton was seated.

His head was turned, so that he could look at Bryce. "I suppose I'd better stay," he said. "We should discuss our plans."

"Sure," Bryce said. "I guess we should." He stood as if frozen for a moment and then he said, hastily, "I . . . I forgot to get ice. For my drink. Excuse me." He went back into the kitchen.

His hand shook as he reached inside the bread drawer and turned on the switch. While the thing was warming up he went to the refrigerator and took ice from the basket. For one of the few times in his life he was grateful for improved technology: thank God it was no longer necessary to fight with ice jammed into stuck trays. He put two cubes in his drink, splashing some of it on his shirt front. Then he went back to the bread drawer, took a deep breath, and pressed the button.

There was an almost imperceptible, momentary hum, and then silence.

He turned the switch off and went back into the living-room. Newton was still in the chair, staring now at the fire. For a while Bryce could not take his eyes from the air-duct, behind which the camera was sitting, its film now exposed.

He shook his head, trying to get the feeling of anxiety out of it. It would be ridiculous to betray himself now that the thing was done. And, he realized, he felt like a traitor—a man who has just betrayed a friend.

Newton said, "I suppose we'll fly."

He couldn't help it. "Like Icarus?" he said, wryly.

Newton laughed. "More like Daedalus, I hope. I wouldn't relish drowning."

It was Bryce's turn now to stand. He did not want to sit and be forced to face Newton. "In your plane?" he said.

"Yes. I thought we would go Christmas morning. That is, if Brinnarde can arrange for space at the airport in Chicago then. I suspect there'll be a rush."

Bryce was finishing his drink—far more quickly than usual, for him. "Not necessarily on Christmas itself," he said. "It's sort of in between the rushed times." Then he said, not knowing exactly why he should ask it, "Will Betty Jo be going along?"

Newton hesitated. "No," he said. "Only the two of us."

He felt a little irrational—as he had felt that other day when the two of them had drunk gin and talked, by the lake. "Won't she miss you?" he asked. It was, of course, none of his business.

"Probably." Newton did not seem offended by the question. "I imagine I'll miss her as well, Doctor Bryce. But she's not going." He looked at the fire a moment longer, in silence. "Can you be ready to leave on Christmas morning at eight o'clock? I'll have Brinnarde pick you up—at the house, if you'd like."

"Fine." Head back, he tossed off the rest of the Scotch. "How long will we be staying?"

"At least two or three days." Newton stood up, began putting on his jacket again. Bryce felt a wave of relief: he had begun to feel as if he could not contain himself any more. The film . . .

"I suppose you'll need a few clean shirts," Newton was saying. "I'll take care of the expenses."

"Why not?" Bryce laughed a little nervously. "You're a millionaire."

"Exactly," Newton said, zipping up his jacket. Bryce was still seated and, looking up, he saw how Newton, sun-tanned and skinny, towered over him like a statue. "Exactly. I'm a millionaire."

Then he left, stooping under the door-sill, and walked lightly out into the snow . . .

His fingers shaking with excitement, and his mind ashamed of the fingers for being so excited, Bryce got the air-duct grill off, took out the camera, set it on the couch, and unloaded it. Then he put on his overcoat, put the film carefully in his pocket, and headed through the snow, which was now quite thick on the ground, for the lab. It was all he could do to keep from running.

The lab was empty—thank God he had chased his assistants out earlier! He headed straight for the developing and projection room. He did not stop to turn on the heaters, although the lab had become very cold. He left his overcoat on.

When he took the negative from the gaseous development bin his hands were shaking so much that it was almost impossible for him to get the film into the machine. But he managed it.

Then, when he turned the switch on the projector, and looked at the screen on the far wall, his hands stopped trembling and the breath caught in his throat. He stared at it for a full minute. Then, abruptly, he turned and walked from the projection room into the lab itself—the huge, long room empty now, and very cold. He was whistling through his teeth, and for some reason the tune was, *If you knew Susie, like I know Susie . . .*

Then, alone in the lab, he began laughing aloud, but softly. "Yes," he said, and the word bounced back at him from the distant wall at the end of the room, bounced back somewhat hollowly, over the test tube racks and Bunsen burners, glassware and crucibles and kilns and testing machines. "Yes," he said, "Yes sir, Rumplestiltskin."

Before he withdrew the film from the projector he stared again at the image on the wall—the image, framed by the faint outline of an armchair, of an impossible bone structure in an impossible body—no sternum, no coccyx, no floating ribs, cartilaginous cervical vertebrae, tiny, pointed scapulae, fused second and third ribs. My God, he thought, my God. Venus, Uranus, Jupiter, Neptune or Mars. My God!

And he saw, down in the corner of the film, the small, hardly noticeable image of the words, W. E. Corp. And their meaning, known to him since he had first inquired about the source of that color film, more than a year before, came back to him with a frightening series of implications: World Enterprises Corporation.

CHAPTER FIVE

THEY TALKED VERY little on the plane. Bryce attempted to read some pamphlets on metallurgical research, but he would find himself fidgeting, his mind wandering. Every now and then he would glance across the narrow lounge to where Newton was sitting, serene, a glass of water in one hand, a book in the other. The book was *The Collected Poetry of Wallace Stevens.* Newton's face was placid; he seemed absorbed. The walls of the lounge were decorated with large colored photographs of water birds—cranes, flamingoes, herons, ducks. The other time he had been aboard the plane, on his first trip to the project site, Bryce had admired the pictures for the taste that had put them there; now they made him feel uncomfortable, seemed almost sinister. Newton sipped his water, turned pages, smiled once or twice toward Bryce, but said nothing. Through a small window behind Newton, Bryce could see a rectangle of dirty gray sky.

It took them a little less than an hour to arrive at Chicago, and another ten minutes to land the plane. They stepped out into a confusion of gray, ambiguous trucks, crowds of determined-looking people, and glassy snow, ridged, re-frozen and dirty. The wind struck his face like a sackful of small needles. He pulled his chin down into his scarf, turned his overcoat collar up, pulled his hat on tighter. As he did this he looked over at Newton. Even Newton seemed affected by the cold wind, for he put his hands in his pockets and winced. Bryce was wearing a heavy overcoat; Newton had on a wool tweed jacket and wool pants. It was strange to see him dressed that way. I wonder what he would look like in a hat, Bryce thought. Maybe a man from Mars should wear a derby.

A snub-nosed truck towed the plane from the field. The graceful little jet seemed to follow the truck sullenly, as if bitter at the ignominy of being on the ground. Someone shouted, "Merry Christmas!" at someone else, and Bryce realized with a start that the day was, indeed, Christmas. Newton passed him, preoccupied, and he began to follow, walking slowly and with care over the plateaus and craters of ice, like dirty gray stone beneath his feet, with a surface like the surface of the moon.

The terminal building was hot, sweaty, noisy, crowded. In the center of the waiting room, stood a gigantic, revolving Christmas tree, made of plastic, covered with plastic snow, plastic icicles, and evil, winking lights. *White Christmas*, sung by an invisible, saccharine choir, with bells and electronic organ, rose, at intervals, above the din of the crowd: "I'm dream-ing of a white Chrisss-mass . . ." That fine old yuletide song. From hidden ducts somewhere was wafted the scent of pine—or of pine oil, like the kind used in public washrooms. Shrill women in furs stood in groups; men walked purposely through the room, carrying briefcases, packages, cameras. A drunk was slumped in an imitation leather armchair, his face blotchy. A child, near Bryce, said to another child, with great intensity, "And you're one, too." Bryce did not catch the reply. "May your days be merry and bright, and may all your Chrisss-massss-esss be whiiite!"

"Our car should be in front of the building," Newton said. Something that suggested pain was in his voice.

Bryce nodded. They walked silently through the crowd and then out the doors. The cold air was a relief.

The car was waiting for them, with a uniformed chauffeur. When they were inside and comfortable, Bryce said, "How do you like Chicago?" Newton looked at him for a moment and said, "I had forgotten about all the people." And then, with a tight smile, he quoted Dante, "'I had not thought death had undone so many.'" Bryce thought, If you're Dante, among the damned—and you probably are—then I'm Virgil.

After lunch in their hotel room they took the elevator to the lobby, where the delegates were milling about, trying to look happy and important and at ease. The lobby was filled with aluminum and mahogany furniture in the Japanese modern style that was the current substitute for elegance. They spent several hours talking to people whom Bryce was fairly acquainted with—and most of whom he did not like—and found three who seemed interested in coming to work for Newton. They made appointments. Newton himself said little. He would nod and smile when introduced, and occasionally make a remark. He attracted some attention—once the word got around who he was—but he seemed not to notice. Bryce got the distinct impression that he was under a considerable strain, yet his face remained as placid as ever.

They were invited to a cocktail party in one of the suites, a tax-deductible affair being given by an engineering firm, and Newton accepted for them. The weasel-faced man who invited them seemed delighted by the acceptance, and said, looking up at Newton, who was a head taller than he, "It'll be a real honor, Mr. Newton. A real honor to have a chance to talk with you."

"Thank you," Newton said, smiling his unvarying smile. Then, when the man was gone, he said to Bryce, "I'd like to take a walk outside now. Would you come along?"

Bryce nodded, relieved. "I'll get my coat."

On his way toward the elevator he passed a group of three men, all well dressed in business suits, talking importantly and loudly. One of them said, as Bryce walked by, ". . . not just in Washington. Why, you can't tell me there's no future in chemical warfare. It's a field that needs new men."

Even though it was Christmas there were stores open. The streets were crowded with people. Most of them had their eyes fixed directly in front of them, their features set. Newton seemed nervous now. He appeared to respond to the presence of people as though they were a wave, or a palpable energy field like that of a thousand electromagnets, about to engulf him. It appeared to require an effort for him to keep moving.

They went into several stores and were assaulted by bright overhead lights and sticky heat. "I think I should buy a gift for Betty Jo," Newton said. Finally, in a jewelry store, he bought her a delicate little clock made of white marble and gold. Bryce carried it back to the hotel for him, in a brightly wrapped box.

"Do you think she'll like it?" Newton said.

Bryce shrugged. "Of course she'll like it."

It was beginning to snow . . .

———————

There were a great number of meetings during the afternoon and evening, but Newton made no mention of them, and Bryce was relieved that he did not have to go to any. He had never had any use for that kind of silliness—discussions of "challenges" and "practicable concepts." They spent the rest of the afternoon interviewing the three men who had shown interest in working for World Enterprises. Two of them accepted jobs to begin in the spring—as well they might, considering the salaries that Newton was paying. One of them would work with coolants for the vehicle's engines; the other, a very bright, affable young man, would work under Bryce. He was a specialist in corrosion. Newton seemed pleased enough to get the two men, but it was also evident that he did not really care. Throughout the interviews he was distracted, vague, and Bryce was forced to do most of the talking. When it was all over Newton seemed relieved. But it was very hard to tell precisely how he felt about anything. It would be interesting to know what went on in that strange, alien mind, and what that automatic smile—that slight, wise, wistful smile—concealed.

The cocktail party was in the penthouse. They entered from the short hallway into a broad, blue-carpeted room, filled with softspoken people, mostly men. One wall of the room was made entirely of glass, and lights from the city were spread across its surface as if painted there in some sort of elaborate molecular diagram. The furniture was entirely Louis Quinze, which Bryce liked. The pictures on the wall were good. A baroque fugue, soft but clear, came from a speaker somewhere; Bryce did not know the piece, but he liked it. Bach? Vivaldi? He liked the room and felt more willing to weather the party for the sake of being in it. Still, there was something incongruous about that glass wall, with Chicago flickering on its surface.

A man detached himself from a group and came to greet them, smiling engagingly. With a start Bryce realized that he was the chemical warfare man from the lobby. He was wearing an excellently tailored black suit, and seemed pleasantly high. "Welcome to our refuge from suburbia," he said, extending his hand. "I'm Fred Benedict. The bar's in there." He nodded conspiratorially toward a doorway.

Bryce took his hand, somewhat annoyed by the calculated firm grip, and introduced himself and Newton.

Benedict was visibly impressed. "Thomas Newton!" he said. "My God, I was hoping you'd come up. You know you've quite a reputation as a . . ." he seemed momentarily embarrassed, "a hermit." He laughed. Newton looked down at him with the same placid smile. Benedict went on, his discomfiture now gone, "Thomas J. Newton—you know it's hard to believe you really exist? My outfit leases seven processes from you—or from World, that is—and the only mental image I've ever had of you has been of some kind of a computer."

"Maybe I am a computing machine," Newton said. And then, "What is your outfit, Mr. Benedict?"

Benedict looked for a moment as if he were afraid he was being mocked. Which, Bryce thought, he probably was.

"I'm with Futures Unlimited. Chemical warfare mostly, although we do some work with plastics—containers and such." He bowed slightly from the waist, in an attempt to be amusing. "Your hosts."

Newton said, "Thank you." He took a step toward the doorway to the bar. "You have a lovely place here."

"We think so. And all deductible." As Newton started to break away, he said, "Let me get your drinks. Mr. Newton. I'd like you to meet some of our guests." He looked as though he wasn't certain what to do with this tall and peculiar man, but was afraid to let him get away.

"Don't bother, Mr. Benedict," Newton said. "We'll rejoin you after a while."

Benedict did not seem pleased, but he made no protest.

Entering the bar room, Bryce said, "I didn't know you were so famous. When I tried to find you, a year ago, no one had ever heard of you."

"You can't keep a secret forever," Newton said, not smiling now.

The room was smaller than the other, but just as elegant. Over the polished bar hung Manet's *Déjeuner sur l'herbe*. The bartender was white haired, elderly, and even more distinguished looking than the scientists and businessmen in the other room. Sitting at the bar Bryce became aware of the shabbiness of his own gray suit, bought at a department store four years before. His shirt, too, he knew, was frayed at the collar, and the sleeves were too long.

He ordered a martini, and Newton ordered plain water with no ice. While the bartender was fixing the drinks, Bryce looked around the room and said, "You know, sometimes I think I should have taken a job with a firm like theirs when I got my doctorate." He laughed dryly. "I could be making eighty thousand a year now and be living like this." He waved his hand out toward the room, letting his eye dwell, for a moment, on a gorgeously dressed, middle-aged woman, with a calculatedly preserved figure and a face that suggested money and pleasure. Green eye shadow, and a mouth for sex. "I could have developed a new kind of plastic for kewpie dolls, or lubricants for outboard motors . . ."

"Or poison gas?" Newton had got his water, and was opening a little silver box, taking out a pill.

"Why not?" He picked up his martini, careful not to spill it. "Somebody has to make the poison gas." He sipped. The drink was so dry it burned his throat and tongue and pushed his voice up a full octave. "Don't they say we need things like poison gas to prevent wars? It's been proved."

"Has it?" Newton said. "Didn't you work somehow with the hydrogen bomb—before you went into teaching?"

"Yes I did. How did you know about that?"

Newton smiled at him—not the automatic smile, but a genuine one of amusement. "I had you investigated."

He took a bigger sip of the drink. "What for? My loyalty?"

"Oh . . . curiosity." He paused for a second, and asked, "Why did you work on the bomb?"

Bryce thought for a minute. Then he laughed at his situation: using a Martian, in a bar, for a confessor. But perhaps it was appropriate. "I didn't know it was going to be a bomb at first," he said. "And in those days I believed in pure science. Reaching for the stars. Secrets of the atom. Our only hope in a chaotic world." He finished the martini.

"And you don't believe those things any more?"

"No."

The music from the other room had changed to a madrigal which he vaguely recognized. It moved delicately, intricately, with the false implication of naiveté that old polyphonic music seemed to have for him. Or was it false? Weren't there naive arts and sophisticated arts? And corrupt arts as well? And might that not be true of the sciences too? Could chemistry be more corrupt than botany? But that wasn't so. It was the uses, the ends . . .

"I don't suppose I do, either," Newton said.

"I think I'll have another martini," Bryce said. A nice, unquestionably corrupt martini. From his mind somewhere came the words, *O ye of little faith.* He laughed to himself, and looked at Newton. Newton sat straight, erect, drinking his water.

The second martini did not burn his throat so much. He ordered a third. After all, the chemical warfare man was paying. Or was it the taxpayers? It depended on how you looked at it. He shrugged. Everybody would pay for all of it anyway—Massachusetts and Mars; everybody everywhere would pay.

"Let's go back in the other room," he said, taking the new martini in his hand, and sipping it cautiously so that it wouldn't spill. His shirt-cuff, he noticed, was entirely out from the end of the coat-sleeve, like a wide and shabby wristband.

As they came through the doorway into the big room their way was blocked by a small, stubby man, talking in slightly drunken agitation. Bryce turned away quickly, hoping the man would not recognize him. He was Walter Canutti from Pendley University, in Pendley, Iowa.

"Bryce!" Canutti said, "Well I'll be damned! Nathan Bryce!"

"Hello, Professor Canutti." He shifted the martini glass to his left hand, awkwardly, and they shook hands. Canutti's face was flushed: he was obviously quite drunk. He was wearing a green silk jacket and a tan shirt, with small, discreet ruffles at the collar. The outfit was much too youthful for him. He looked, except for the pink, soft face, like a mannequin on the cover of a men's fashion magazine. Bryce tried to keep the revulsion from showing in his voice. "Nice to see you again!"

Canutti was looking questioningly at Newton, and there was nothing to do but introduce them. Bryce stumbled through the names, enraged at himself for being awkward.

Canutti was, if anything, more impressed with Newton's name than the other man, Benedict, had been. He pumped Newton's hand with both of his, saying, "Yes. Yes, of course. World Enterprises. Biggest thing since General Dynamics." He was laying it on as if he were hoping for a fat research contract for Pendley. It always horrified Bryce to see professors fawn on businessmen—the very men they ridiculed in their private conversations—whenever a research contract might be in the offing.

Newton murmured and smiled, and finally Canutti released his hand, made an attempt at a boyish grin, and said, *"Well!"* And then, throwing his arm over Bryce's shoulder, "Well, it's a lot of water under the bridge, Nate." Abruptly, a thought seemed to strike him, and Bryce winced inwardly in apprehension. Canutti looked at both of them, Bryce and Newton, and said, "Why, are you working for World Enterprises, Nate?"

He didn't answer, knowing what would be coming next.

Then Newton said, "Doctor Bryce has been with us for over a year."

"Well I'll be ..." Canutti's face was reddening, above the frilled collar. "Well I'll be damned. Working for World Enterprises!" A look of uncontrollable mirth spread across his chubby face, and Bryce, drinking off his martini at a gulp, felt that he could readily plant a heel into that face. The grin became a belching chuckle, and then Canutti turned to Newton and said, "This is priceless. I've got to tell you this, Mr. Newton." He chuckled again. "I'm sure Nate won't mind, because it's all over now. But do you know, Mr. Newton, when Nate left us out at Pendley he was worrying his head off about some of the very things that he's probably helping you make, over at World?"

"Really?" Newton said, filling the pause.

"But the clincher is this." Canutti reached a fumbling hand out and laid it on Bryce's shoulder. Bryce felt as though he could have bitten it off, but he listened, fascinated, at what he knew was coming.

"The clincher is that old Nate here thought you were producing all that stuff you make by some kind of voodoo. Right, Nate?"

"That's right," Bryce said. "Voodoo."

Canutti laughed. "Nate's one of the top men in the field, as I'm sure you know, Mr. Newton. But maybe it was going to his head. He thought your color films were invented on Mars."

"Oh?" Newton said.

"That's right. Mars or somewhere. 'Extraterrestrial' is what he said." Canutti squeezed Bryce's shoulder, to show he meant no harm. "I bet when he saw you he expected somebody with three heads. Or tentacles."

Newton smiled cordially. "That's very amusing." Then he looked at Bryce. "I'm sorry I disappointed you," he said.

Bryce looked away. "No disappointment at all," he said. His hands were trembling, and he set his glass on a table, forced his hands into his jacket pockets.

Canutti was talking again, this time about some magazine article he'd read, something about World Enterprises and its contributions to the gross national product. Abruptly, Bryce interrupted. "Excuse me," he said. "I think I'll get another drink." Then he turned and went quickly back into the room with the bar, not looking at either of the other two as he did so.

But when he got his drink he did not want it. The bar had become oppressive to him; the bartender no longer looked distinguished but seemed merely a pretentious flunky. The music from the other room—now a motet—was nervous and shrill. There were too many people in the bar, and their voices were too loud. He looked around him, as if in desperation: the men were all sleek, smug; the women were like harpies. *To hell with it*, he thought, *to hell with it all.* He pushed himself from the bar, leaving his untouched drink, and walked purposely back into the main room.

Newton was waiting for him, alone.

Bryce looked him directly in the eyes, trying not to flinch. "Where's Canutti?" he said.

"I told him we were leaving." He shrugged his shoulders, in the implausible French gesture that Bryce had seen him use before. "He's an offensive man, isn't he?"

Bryce kept looking up at him for a moment, at his untranslatable eyes. Then he said, "Let's get out of here."

They left in silence and walked side by side, saying nothing, down the long, heavily-carpeted hallway to their room. Bryce unlocked the door with his key, and after he had closed it behind them he said, quietly now, his voice steady, "Well, are you?"

Newton sat on the edge of the bed, smiled wearily at him, and said, "Of course I am."

There was nothing to say. Bryce found himself muttering, "Jesus Christ. Jesus Christ." He seated himself in an armchair, and stared at his feet. "Jesus Christ."

He sat there for what seemed like a long time, staring at his feet. He had known it, but the shock of hearing it said was another thing.

Then Newton spoke. "Do you want something to drink?"

He looked up and, suddenly, laughed. "God, yes."

Newton reached for the bedside phone and called room service. He asked for two bottles of gin, vermouth, and ice. Then, hanging up the receiver, he said, "Let's get drunk, Doctor Bryce. It's an occasion."

They did not talk until the bellboy came, bringing a cart with the liquor and ice and a martini pitcher. On the tray was a dish of cocktail onions, lemon peel, and green olives. Another dish had nuts in it. When the boy had left, Newton said, "Would you mind fixing the drinks? I'd like plain gin." He was still sitting on the edge of the bed.

"Sure." Bryce got up, feeling light-headed. "Is it Mars?"

Newton's voice seemed peculiar. Or was it only that he, Bryce, was drunk? "Does it make any difference?"

"I'm sure it does. Are you from this . . . solar system?"

"Yes. As far as I know, there aren't any others."

"No other solar systems?"

Newton took the glass of gin that Bryce offered him, and held it, speculatively. "Only suns," he said, "no planets. Or none that I know of."

Bryce was stirring a martini. His hands were perfectly steady now; he had passed over some kind of hump. He felt as though nothing further could touch him, could shake him. "How long have you been here?" he said, stirring, listening to the ice clink against the side of the pitcher.

"Haven't you mixed that drink enough?" Newton said. "You'd better drink it." He took a swallow from his own. "I've been on your Earth five years."

Bryce stopped stirring the drink, poured it into a glass. Then, feeling expansive, he dropped in three olives. Some of the martini splashed out on to the white linen cover of the cart, making wet spots. "Do you intend to stay?" he said. It sounded as though he were in a Paris café, asking the question of another tourist. Newton should be wearing a camera around his neck.

"Yes, I intend to stay."

Seated now, Bryce found his vision wandering around the room. It was a pleasant room, with pale green walls and innocuous pictures hung on them.

He refocused his gaze on Newton. Thomas Jerome Newton, from Mars. Mars or somewhere. "Are you human?" he said.

Newton's drink was half empty. "A matter of definition," he said. "I'm human enough, however."

He started to ask, *Human enough for what?* but did not. He might as well get down to the second big question, since he had already asked the first. "What are you here for?" he said. "What are you up to?"

Newton stood up, poured some more gin in his glass, walked to an armchair, sat down. He looked at Bryce, holding the glass delicately in his slender hand. "I'm not certain that I know what I'm up to," he said.

"Not certain that you know?" Bryce said.

Newton set his glass on the table by the bed and began taking off his shoes. "I thought I knew what I was here for, at first. But then, for the first two years I was busy, very busy. I've had more time to think, this past year. Possibly too much time." He set his shoes neatly, side by side, under the bed. Then he stretched his long legs out on the bedspread and leaned against the pillow.

He certainly *looked* human enough, in that pose. "What is the ship being built for? It is a ship, isn't it, and not just an exploratory device?"

"It's a ship. Or, more precisely, a ferry boat."

For some time, ever since the talk with Canutti, Bryce had felt stunned: everything had seemed unreal. But now he was beginning to regain his grasp of things, and the scientist in him was beginning to assert itself. He set his glass down, deciding not to drink any more just now. It was important to keep a clear head. But his hand, as it put down the glass, was shaking.

"Then you're planning to bring more of your . . . people here? On the ferry?"

"Yes."

"Are there any more of you here?"

"I'm the only one."

"But why build your ship here? Certainly you must have them where you came from. You got here yourself."

"Yes, I got here. But in a one-man craft. The problem, you see, is fuel. There was only enough to send one of us, and only on one crossing."

"Atomic fuel? Uranium or something?"

"Yes. Of course. But we have almost none left. Nor do we have petroleum, or coal, or hydro-electric power." He smiled. "There are probably hundreds of ships, much superior to the one we are building in Kentucky; but there was no way to get them here. None of them has been used for over five hundred of your years. The one I came on was not even intended as an interplanetary vessel. It was originally designed as an emergency craft—a lifeboat. I destroyed the engines and the controls after landing, and left the hull in a field. I've read in the newspapers that there's a farmer who charges people fifty cents to see it. He has it in a tent, and sells soft drinks. I wish him well."

"Isn't there some danger in that?"

"Of my being found out by the FBI or someone? I don't think so. The worst to happen was some Sunday supplement nonsense about possible invaders from outer space. But there have been more surprising curiosities for Sunday paper readers than spaceship hulls found in Kentucky minefields. I don't think anyone of importance has taken it seriously."

Bryce looked at him closely. "Is 'invaders from outer space' only nonsense?"

Newton unbuttoned his shirt collar. "I think so."

"Then what are your people coming here for? As tourists?"

Newton laughed. "Not exactly. We might be able to help you."

"How?" Somehow he did not like the way Newton had said it. "How help us?"

"We might be able to save you from destroying yourselves, if we are quick enough about it." Then, when Bryce started to speak, he said, "Let me talk for a while. I don't think you know what a pleasure it gives me to talk about it—to talk at length." He had not picked his glass up again, after getting in bed. He folded his hands over his stomach, and, looking gently at Bryce, went on. "We've had our own wars, you see. A great many more than you have had, and we have only barely survived them. That's where most of our radio-active materials went, into bombs. We used to be a very powerful people, very powerful; but that has been over for a long time. Now we barely survive." He looked down at his hands, as if in speculation. "It's a strange thing that most of your imaginative literature about life on the other planets always assumes that each planet would have only one intelligent race, one type of society, one language, one government. On Anthea—our name is Anthea, although, of course, that is not the name in your astronomy books—we had, at one time, three intelligent species and seven major governments. Now there is only one species left of any consequence, and that is my own. We are the survivors, after five wars fought with radio-active weapons. And there are not very many of us. But we know a great deal about warfare. And we have a great deal of technical knowledge." Newton's eyes were still fixed on his hands; his voice had assumed a monotone, as if he were reciting a prepared speech. "I have been here five years, and I own property worth more than three hundred million dollars. In five more years it will be double that. And that is only a beginning. If the plan is carried out there will eventually be the equivalent of World Enterprises in every major country of this world. Then we will go into politics. And the military. We know about weapons and defenses. Yours are still crude. We can, for instance, render radar impotent— a thing quite necessary when I landed my craft here and more necessary when the ferry boat returns. We can also generate an energy system that will prevent the detonation of any of your nuclear weapons within a five-mile radius."

"Is that enough?"

"I don't know. But my superiors aren't stupid, and they seem to think it can be done. As long as we keep our devices and our knowledge under our own control, building up the economy of one small country here, buying a critical food surplus there, starting an industry somewhere else, giving one nation a weapon, and another a defense against it . . ."

"But, damn it, you're not gods."

"No. But have your gods ever saved you before?"

"I don't know. No, of course not." Bryce lit a cigarette. It took three tries: his hands refused to hold steady. He inhaled deeply, trying to calm himself. He felt somehow like a college sophomore, arguing human destiny. But this was not exactly abstract philosophizing. "Doesn't mankind have a right to choose its own form of destruction?" he said.

Newton waited a moment before he spoke. "Do you really believe that mankind does have such a right?"

Bryce ground his cigarette, only partly smoked, into the ashtray beside him. "Yes. No. I don't know. Isn't there such a thing as human destiny? The right to fulfill ourselves, to live out our own lives and take our own consequences?" Saying this it suddenly struck him that Newton was the only link with—what was it?—Anthea. If Newton were destroyed there could be no carrying out of that plan: it would all be over. And Newton was frail, very frail. The thought held him fascinated for a minute; he, Bryce, was potentially the hero of all heroes—the man who could, with a heavy blow from his fist, probably save the world. This could have been very amusing; but it was not.

"There may be such a thing as human destiny," Newton said, "but I rather imagine it resembles passenger-pigeon destiny. Or the destiny of those large creatures with small brains—I think they were called dinosaurs."

That seemed a little supercilious. "We won't necessarily become extinct. Disarmament is being negotiated. Not all of us are insane."

"But most of you are. Enough of you are—it only requires a few insane ones, in the right places. Suppose your man Hitler had been in possession of fusion bombs and intercontinental missiles? Wouldn't he have used them, regardless of the consequences? He had nothing to lose toward the end."

"How do I know that your Antheans won't be Hitlers?"

Newton looked away. "It's possible, but unlikely."

"Do you come from a democratic society?"

"We have nothing resembling a democratic society on Anthea. Nor do we have democratic social institutions. But we have no intention of ruling you, even if we could."

"Then what do you call it," Bryce said, "if you plan to have a bunch of Antheans manipulating men and governments all over the earth?"

"We could call it what you just called it—manipulation, or guidance. And it might not work. It might not work at all. You might blow your world apart first, or you might find us out and begin a witch hunt—we are vulnerable, you know. Or, even if we do get a large measure of power, we cannot control every accident. But we can reduce the probability of Hitlers, and we can protect your major cities from destruction. And that," he shrugged, "is more than you can do."

"And you want to do this just to help us?" Bryce heard the sarcasm in his voice, and hoped that Newton did not notice.

If Newton had noticed he gave no sign of it. "Of course not. We are coming here to save ourselves. But," he smiled, "we do not want the Indians burning up our reservation after we have settled on it."

"What are you saving yourselves from?"

"Extinction. We have almost no water, no fuel, no natural resources. We have feeble solar power—feeble because we are so far from the sun—and we still have large stores of food. But they are dwindling. There are less than three hundred Antheans alive."

"Less than three hundred? My God, you did almost wipe yourselves out!"

"We did indeed. As, I imagine, you will do before long, if we don't come."

"Maybe you should come," he said. "Maybe you should." Bryce felt a tenseness in his throat. "But if something should . . . happen to you, before the ship is complete? Wouldn't that be the end of it?"

"Yes. That would end it."

"No fuel for another ship?"

"No fuel."

"Then," Bryce said, feeling himself tense, "what is to prevent me from stopping this—this invasion, or manipulation? Shouldn't I kill you? You're very weak, I know. I imagine your bones are like a bird's, from what Betty Jo told me."

Newton's face was completely undisturbed. "Do you want to stop it? You're quite right: you could snap my neck like a chicken's. Do you want to? Now that you know my name is Rumplestiltskin do you want to drive me from the palace?"

"I don't know." He looked at the floor.

Newton's voice was soft. "Rumplestiltskin did weave straw into gold."

Bryce looked up, suddenly angry. "Yes. And he tried to steal the princess's child."

"Of course he did," Newton said. "But if he hadn't woven the straw into gold the princess would have died. And there would not have been any child at all."

"All right," Bryce said. "I won't wring your neck to save the world."

"Do you know?" said Newton, "I almost wish, now, that you could. It would make things much simpler for me." He paused. "But you can't."

"Why can't I?"

"I didn't come to your world unprepared for discovery. Although I did not expect to be telling anyone what I have told you. But there was a great deal I did not expect." He looked down at his hands again, seeming to examine the nails. "In any event, I am carrying a weapon. I always carry it."

"An Anthean weapon?"

"Yes. A very effective one. You would never have made it across the floor to my bed."

Bryce inhaled rapidly. "How does it work?"

Newton grinned. "Does Macy's tell Gimbel's?" he said. "I may have to use it on you yet."

A quality in the way that Newton had just spoken—not the ironic or pseudo-sinister quality of the statement itself, but some minor strangeness in the manner—reminded Bryce that he was, after all, talking to someone not human. The practiced veneer of humanness that Newton assumed might be merely that: a very thin veneer. Whatever was beneath the veneer, the essential part of Newton, his specifically Anthean nature, might very well be inaccessible to him, Bryce, or for that matter to anyone on Earth. The way that Newton actually felt or thought might be beyond his comprehension, totally unavailable to him.

"Whatever your weapon is," he spoke more carefully now, "I hope you won't have to use it." And then he looked around him again, at the big hotel room, the almost untouched tray of liquor, and back at Newton, reclining in bed. "My God," he said, "it's hard to believe. To sit in this room and believe that I'm talking to a man from another planet."

"Yes," Newton said, "I've thought that myself. I'm talking to a man from another planet too, you know."

Bryce stood up and stretched. Then he walked to the window, parted the draperies, looked down at the street. Car headlights were everywhere, hardly moving. A huge, illu-

minated billboard directly across from the hotel showed
Santa Claus drinking a Coca-Cola. Clusters of flickering
bulbs made Santa's eyes twinkle, made the soft drink sparkle.
Somewhere, faintly, Bryce could hear chimes playing *Adeste
Fideles.*

He turned back to Newton, who had not moved. "Why
have you told me? You didn't have to."

"I wanted to tell you." He smiled. "I haven't been at all sure
of my motives for the past year; I'm not certain why I wanted
to tell you. Antheans don't necessarily know everything. Anyway, you already knew about me."

"Are you talking about what Canutti said? That might have
been only a stab in the dark on my part. It might have been
nothing."

"I wasn't thinking of what Professor Canutti said. Although
I found your reaction to it amusing: I thought you might have
a stroke of apoplexy when he said 'Mars.' But his saying that
forced your hand, not mine."

"Why not yours?"

"Well, Doctor Bryce, there are a great many differences
between you and me of which you could hardly be aware. One
of them is that my vision is much more acute than yours, and
its effective range of frequencies is considerably higher. This
means that I cannot see the color that you call 'red.' But I can
see X-rays."

Bryce opened his mouth to speak, but then said nothing.

"Once I had seen the flash," Newton said, "it wasn't difficult to determine what you were doing." He looked at Bryce
inquisitively. "How was the picture?"

Bryce felt foolish, like a trapped schoolboy. "The picture
was . . . remarkable."

Newton nodded. "I can imagine. If you could see my internal organs you would have some surprises too. I went to a natural history museum once, in New York. A very interesting place for a . . . for a tourist. It occurred to me there that I myself was the only truly unique biological specimen in the building. I could picture myself pickled, in a jar, with the label, *Extraterrestrial humanoid*. I left rather quickly."

Bryce could not help laughing. And, Newton, now that he had, as it were, made his confession, seemed expansive, seemed paradoxically even more "human," now that he had made it clear that he was, in fact, no such thing. His face was more expressive, his manner more relaxed, than Bryce had ever seen them. But there was still that hint of another Newton, a thoroughly Anthean Newton, unapproachable and alien. "Do you plan to go back to your planet?" Bryce said. "On the ship?"

"No. It won't be necessary. The ship will be guided from Anthea itself. I'm afraid I'm a permanent exile here."

"Do you miss your . . . your own people?"

"I miss them."

Bryce walked back to his chair and seated himself again. "But you will be seeing them before long?"

Newton hesitated. "Possibly."

"Why possibly? Something might go wrong?"

"I wasn't thinking about that." And then, "I told you earlier that I was not at all certain what I was up to."

Bryce looked at him, puzzled. "I don't understand what you mean."

"Well," Newton smiled faintly, "for some time now I have been considering not completing the plan, not sending the ship anywhere—not even finishing the construction. It would only require a single order."

"For God's sake, why?"

"Oh, the plan was an intelligent one, although desperate. But what else could we do?" Newton was looking at him, but did not seem to be seeing him. "However, I have developed some doubts about its final worth. There are things about your culture here, your society, that we did not know about on Anthea. Do you know, Doctor Bryce," he shifted his position in the bed, leaning over closer to Bryce, "that I sometimes think that I will be insane in a few more years? I'm not certain that my people will be able to stand your world. We've been in an ivory tower for a long time."

"But you could isolate yourselves from the world. You have money; you could stay with your own, build your own society." What was he doing—defending the Anthean...invasion? After he had just been frightened and stunned by it? "You could make your own city, in Kentucky."

"And wait for the bombs to fall? We would be better off on Anthea. There at least we can live for another fifty years. If we are to live here, it won't be as an isolated colony of freaks. We'll have to disperse ourselves over your entire world, place ourselves in positions of influence. Otherwise it would be foolish for us to come."

"Whatever you do you'll be taking a great risk. Can't you gamble on our solving our own problems, if you are afraid of close contact with us?" He smiled wryly. "Be our guests."

"Doctor Bryce," Newton said, his face now unsmiling, "we are a great deal wiser than you are. Believe me, we are much wiser than you may imagine. And we are certain beyond all reasonable doubt that your world will be an atomic rubble heap in no more than thirty years, if you are left to yourselves." He continued grimly, "To tell you the truth, it dismays us greatly to see what you are about to do with such a beautiful, fertile world. We destroyed ours a long time ago, but we had so much less to begin with than you have here." His voice now seemed agitated, his manner more intense. "Do you realize that you will not only wreck your civilization, such as it is, and kill most of your people; but that you will also poison the fish in your rivers, the squirrels in your trees, the flocks of birds, the soil, the water? There are times when you seem, to us, like apes loose in a museum, carrying knives, slashing the canvases, breaking the statuary with hammers."

For a moment Bryce did not speak. Then he said, "But it was human beings who painted the pictures, made the statues."

"Only a few human beings," Newton said. "Only a few." Abruptly, he stood up and said, "I think I've had quite enough of Chicago. Would you like to go home?"

"*Now?*" Bryce looked at his watch. My God, two-thirty in the morning. Christmas was over.

"Do you think you'll sleep tonight anyway?" Newton said.

He shrugged, "I guess not." And then, remembering what Betty Jo had said, "You don't sleep at all, do you?"

"Sometimes I sleep," Newton said, "but not often." He sat down beside the telephone. "I'll have to have our pilot wakened. And we'll need a car to take us to the airport . . ."

Getting a car was difficult; they did not arrive at the airport until four o'clock. By that time Bryce was beginning to feel dizzy, and there was a faint buzzing in his ears. Newton showed no signs of fatigue. His face, as usual, gave no indication of what he might be thinking.

There were confusions and several delays in getting take-off clearance, and by the time they were able to leave, flying out over Lake Michigan, a pink and gentle dawn was beginning to form.

It was daylight when they arrived in Kentucky, the beginning of a clear winter day. Coming in for the landing the first thing they saw was the brilliantly shining hull of the ship—Newton's ferry boat—looking like a polished monument in the morning sun. And then, when they came over the airfield they saw a surprising thing. Perched elegantly at the far end of the runway, at the side of Newton's hangar, was a beautifully streamlined, white airplane, twice the size of the one they were in. On its wings were the markings of the United States Air Force. "Well," Newton said, "I wonder who has come to visit us."

They had to walk by the white plane on their way to the monorail, and, passing it, Bryce could not help being impressed with its beauty—its fine proportions and the grace of its lines. "If we only made everything that beautifully," he said.

Newton was looking at the plane, too. "But you don't," he said.

They rode the monorail car in silence. Bryce's arms and legs ached with the need for sleep; but his mind was full of sharp, quick images, ideas, half-formed thoughts.

He should have gone to his own house; but when Newton invited him in for breakfast, he accepted. It would be easier than finding his own food.

Betty Jo was up, wearing an orange kimono, her hair in a silk babushka; her face was worried, and her eyes were red, puffy underneath. Opening the door she said, "There's some men here, Mr. Newton. I don't know . . ." Her voice trailed off. They went past her into the living-room. Seated in chairs were five men; they rose quickly when Newton and Bryce entered.

Brinnarde was in the center of the group. There were three other men in business suits, and the fourth, wearing a blue uniform, was obviously the pilot of the Air Force plane. Brinnarde introduced them, his manner efficient, non-committal. When this was done, Newton, still standing, said, "Have you been waiting long?"

"No," Brinnarde said, "no. In fact we had you delayed at the Chicago airport until we could get here. The timing was very good. I hope you weren't inconvenienced too much—by the hold-up at Chicago?"

Newton showed no emotion. "How did you manage to do that?"

"Well, Mr. Newton," Brinnarde said, "I'm with the Federal Bureau of Investigation. These men are my colleagues."

Newton's voice hesitated slightly. "That's very interesting. I suppose it makes you a . . . a spy?"

"I suppose it does. In any event, Mr. Newton, I've been told to place you under arrest, and to take you with me."

Newton took a slow, deep, very human breath. "What are you arresting me for?"

Brinnarde smiled politely. "You're charged with illegal entry. We believe you're an alien, Mr. Newton."

Newton stood silent for a long moment. Then he said, "May I have breakfast first, please?"

Brinnarde hesitated, then he smiled in a way that was surprisingly genial. "I don't see why not, Mr. Newton," he said. "I think we could use some food ourselves. They got up at four this morning, in Louisville, to make this arrest."

Betty Jo fixed them scrambled eggs and coffee. While they were eating, Newton asked casually if he could call his lawyer.

"I'm afraid not," Brinnarde said.

"Isn't there a constitutional right about that?"

"Yes." Brinnarde set down his coffee cup. "But you don't have any constitutional rights. As I said, we believe that you are not an American citizen."

CHAPTER SIX

NEWTON PUT DOWN his book. The doctor would be coming in a few minutes, and he did not feel like reading anyway. In the two weeks of his confinement he had done very little but read. That was when he wasn't being questioned, or examined by the doctors—physicians, anthropologists, psychiatrists—or by the men in conservative suits who must have been government officials, although they would never tell him who they were when he asked. He had re-read Spinoza, Hegel, Spengler, Keats, the New Testament, and was currently reading some new books on linguistics. They brought him whatever he asked for, with considerable speed and politeness. He also had a record player, which he seldom used, a library of motion picture films, a World Enterprises television set, and a bar, but no windows to look through to see Washington. They had told him he was someplace near that city, although they were not specific about how near he was. He watched the television set in the evenings, partly from a kind of nostalgia, sometimes from curiosity. At times his name would be mentioned on news programs—for it was impossible that a man of his wealth could have been placed under arrest by the government without some publicity. But the references were always vague, coming from unnamed official sources and making use of phrases like "a cloud of suspicion." The word was that he was an "unregistered alien"; but no government source had made it plain where he was—or where they thought he was—from. One television commentator, noted for his dry wit, had said waspishly, "For all that Washington will say, it must be assumed that Mr. Newton, now under surveillance and in custody, is a visitor either from Outer Mongolia or from outer space."

He realized, too, that these broadcasts would be monitored by his superiors on Anthea, and he was mildly amused by the thought of their consternation at learning of his position, their curiosity to find out what was really happening.

Well, he did not know himself what was really happening. Apparently the government was highly suspicious of him—as well they might be, with the information that Brinnarde must have given them during the year and a half that he had been working as his secretary. And Brinnarde, who had been his right-hand man on the project, must certainly have placed a good many spies in all aspects of the organization, so that the government should have in hand a great deal of information about his activities and about the project itself. But there had been things he had kept from Brinnarde, things they were highly unlikely to know about. Still, it was impossible to determine what they were up to. Sometimes he wondered what would happen if he told his questioners, "As a matter of fact I am from outer space, and I intend to conquer the world." It might produce interesting reactions. But belief would hardly be one of them.

Sometimes he wondered what was happening to World Enterprises, now that he was entirely cut off from communication with it. Would Farnsworth be running it? Newton received no mail, no phone calls. There was a telephone in his living-room, but it never rang, and he was not permitted to make outside calls on it. The phone was pale blue, and it sat on a mahogany table. He had tried it a few times, but always a voice—apparently a recorded voice—would say, when he picked it up, "We are sorry, but this telephone is restricted." The voice was pleasant, feminine, artificial. It never said what the telephone was restricted to. Sometimes, when lonely, or a little bit drunk—he did not drink so much as before, now that some of the pressure was removed from him—he would pick up the receiver just to hear the voice say, "We are sorry, but this telephone is restricted." The voice was very smooth; it suggested infinite politeness and some dim kind of electronics.

The doctor was punctual as ever: the guard let him in at exactly eleven o'clock. He carried his bag and was accompanied by a nurse with a deliberately impassive face—the sort of face that seemed to say, "I don't care what you die of, I intend to be efficient about my part of it." She was a blonde, and by human standards, pretty. The doctor's name was Martinez; he was a physiologist.

"Good morning, Doctor," Newton said. "What can I do for you?"

The doctor smiled with practiced casualness. "Another test, Mr. Newton. Another small test." He had a faint Spanish accent. Newton rather liked him; he was less formal than most of the people he had to deal with.

"I should think you'd know all you wish to about me by now," Newton said. "You've X-rayed me, sampled my blood and lymph, recorded my brain waves, measured me, and taken direct samples from my bone, liver and kidneys. I hardly think I'd have any more surprises for you."

The doctor shook his head and granted Newton a perfunctory laugh. "God knows we've found you . . . interesting. You have a rather far-fetched set of organs."

"I'm a freak, Doctor."

The doctor laughed again; but his laugh was strained. "I don't know what we'd do if you developed appendicitis or something. We'd hardly know where to look."

Newton smiled at him. "You wouldn't have to bother. I don't have an appendix." He leaned back in his chair. "But I imagine you'd operate anyway. You would probably be delighted to open me up and see what new curiosities you could find."

"Oh, I don't know," the doctor said. "As a matter of fact, one of the first things we learned about you—after counting your toes, that is—was that you have no vermiform appendix. In fact there are many things you don't have. We've been using rather advanced equipment, you know." Then, abruptly, he turned to the nurse. "Will you give Mr. Newton the Nembucaine, Miss Griggs?"

Newton winced. "Doctor," he said, "I've told you before that anesthetics have no effect on my nervous system, except to give me a headache. If you are going to do something painful to me there is no point in making it more painful."

The nurse, ignoring him completely, began preparing a

hypodermic. Doctor Martinez gave the patronizing smile evidently reserved for patients' fumbling efforts to understand the rites of medicine. "Maybe you're unaware of how much these things would hurt if we didn't use anesthetics."

Newton was beginning to feel exasperated. His sense of being an intelligent human besieged by curious and pompous monkeys had become very acute during the past weeks. Except, of course, that it was he in the cage, while the monkeys came and went, examining him and attempting to appear wise. "Doctor," he said, "haven't you seen the results of the intelligence tests given me?"

The doctor had opened his brief-case on the desk and was removing some forms. Each sheet was clearly stamped, Top Secret. "Intelligence tests aren't in my bailiwick, Mr. Newton. And as you probably know, all of that information is highly confidential."

"Yes. But you do know."

The doctor cleared his throat. He was beginning to fill in one of the forms. Date; type of test. "Well, there have been some rumors."

Newton was angry now. "I imagine there have been. I also imagine that you are aware that my intelligence is about twice yours. Can't you credit me with knowing whether or not local anesthetic is effective for me?"

"We've studied the arrangement of your nervous system exhaustively. There seems to be no reason why Nembucaine wouldn't work as well for you as for . . . as for anybody."

"Maybe you don't know as much about nervous systems as you think you do."

"That may be." The doctor had finished with the form, and

set his pencil on it for a paper-weight. An unnecessary paper-weight, since there were no windows and no breeze. "That may be. But again, it's not my bailiwick."

Newton glanced at the nurse, who had the needle ready. She seemed to be making an effort to appear unaware of their conversation. He wondered, briefly, how they would go about keeping such people silent about their curious prisoner, keeping them away from reporters—or, for that matter, away from bridge games with friends. Maybe the government kept everyone who worked on him in isolation. But that would be difficult and awkward. Still, they were obviously taking great pains with him. He found it almost amusing that he must be the occasion of some wild speculation among the few people who knew of his peculiarities.

"What is your bailiwick, Doctor?" he said.

The doctor shrugged. "Bones and muscles, mostly."

"That sounds pleasant." The doctor took the needle from the nurse and Newton, resigning himself, began rolling up his shirt-sleeve.

"You might as well take the shirt off," the doctor said. "We'll be working on your back, this time."

He did not protest, but began unbuttoning the shirt. When he had it half-way off he heard the nurse catch her breath softly. He looked up at her. Obviously they hadn't told her much, since what she was carefully trying not to stare at was his chest, bare of hair and nipples. They had, of course, found out his disguises early, and he wore them no longer. He wondered what the nurse's reaction would be when she got close enough to him to notice the pupils of his eyes.

When he had the shirt off the nurse injected him in the muscles on each side of his spine. She attempted to be gentle, but the pain was, for him, considerable. After that part of it was over he said, "Now what are you going to do?"

The doctor noted the time of the injection on his form sheet. Then he said, "First, I'm going to wait twenty minutes while the Nembucaine . . . takes effect. Then I'm going to draw samples from the marrow of your spinal vertebrae."

Newton looked at him a moment, silently. Then he said, "Haven't you learned yet? There is no marrow in my bones. They are hollow."

The doctor blinked. "Come now," he said, "there must be bone marrow. The red corpuscles of the blood—"

Newton was not accustomed to interrupting people; but he interrupted this time. "I don't know about the red corpuscles and the marrow. I probably know as much about physiology as you do. But there is no marrow in my bones. And I can't say that I will enjoy submitting to some painful probing on your part so that you—or whoever your superiors might be— can satisfy yourselves as to my . . . peculiarities. I've told you a dozen times that I'm a mutant—a freak. Can't you take my word for anything?"

"I'm sorry," the doctor said. He looked as though he were sorry.

Newton stared past the doctor's head for a moment, at a bad reproduction of Van Gogh's *Woman of Arles*. What could the United States Government have to do with a woman of Arles? "Someday I'd like to meet your superiors," he said. "And while we're waiting for your ineffective Nembucaine to take effect, I'd like to try an anesthetic of my own."

The doctor's face was blank.

"Gin," Newton said. "Gin and water. Would you like to join me?"

The doctor smiled automatically. All good doctors smile at the witticisms of their patients—even research physiologists of well checked loyalty are supposed to smile. "I'm sorry," he said. "I'm on duty now."

Newton was surprised at his own exasperation. And he had thought he liked Doctor Martinez. "Come now, Doctor. I'm certain you're a very expensive practitioner of your . . . of your bailiwick, with a mahogany-veneered bar in your office. And I can assure you, I wouldn't give you enough alcohol to cause your hand to tremble while you're probing my spine."

"I don't have an office," the doctor said. "I work in a laboratory. We don't normally drink on the job."

Newton, for some unaccountable reason, stared at him. "No, I don't suppose you do." He looked at the nurse, but when she, now visibly rattled, opened her mouth to speak, he said, "No, I suppose not. Regulations." Then he stood up and smiled down at them. "I'll drink alone." It was nice to be taller than they were. He walked to the bar in the corner and poured himself a tumbler full of gin. He decided to omit the water, since, while he had been talking, the nurse had been laying a set of instruments on a sheet that she had spread over the table. There were several needles, a small knife, and some kind of clamps, all made of stainless steel. They glittered prettily . . .

After the doctor and nurse had gone he lay face down on his bed for over an hour. He did not put his shirt on again, and his back, except for the bandages, was still bare. He felt faintly cold—an unusual sensation for him—but made no move to cover himself. The pain had been very intense for several minutes, and, although it was over now, he was exhausted by it and by the fear that had preceded it. He had always been frightened by the anticipation of pain, ever since his childhood.

It had occurred to him that they might know the pain they were causing him, that they might be torturing him in some ill-conceived form of brainwashing, in the hope of breaking his mind. The thought was especially frightening, for if that were so they would only just have begun. But it was very unlikely. Despite the excuse of the perpetual cold war, and despite the very real tyranny that was tolerated in a democracy at such times—it would be too difficult for them to get away with it. And the year was an election year. Already there had been campaign speeches alluding to the high-handedness of the party in power. In one such speech his name had been mentioned. The word "cover-up" was used several times.

The only logical reason for submitting him to the painful tests must be some form of bureaucratic curiosity. Probably the justification was their desire to prove conclusively that he was non-human, to prove that he was indeed what they must have suspected he was—suspected, but could not admit to, because of its absurdity. If that was the way their thinking went, and very likely it was, they were in very obvious error from the outset. For, no matter what non-human attributes they might find, it would always be more plausible that he was a human physical deviate, a mutation, sport, freak, than that he was from some other planet. Still, they did not seem to see this difficulty. What could they hope to find out in detail that they didn't already know, in general? And what could they prove? And, finally, if proved beyond doubt, what then could they do?"

But he did not care very much—did not care what they found out about him, did not even care very much what happened to that old, old plan, conceived twenty years before in

another part of the solar system. He supposed, without thinking about it very much, that it was all over anyway, and he felt
little more than relief. What he cared most about was that they
would get their infernal experiments and tests and questions
done with, and leave him alone. Being imprisoned as he was,
was no problem for him—in many ways it was more native to
his way of life, and more satisfying, than freedom.

CHAPTER SEVEN

THE FBI WAS polite and gentle enough, but after two days of nonsensical questions, Bryce was profoundly weary, unable even to feel anger at the contempt he could sense behind their politeness. Had they not released him on the third day, he felt that he might have gone to pieces. Yet they hadn't put him under any noticeable strain; in fact they hardly seemed to consider him important.

On the third morning the man came, as usual, to pick him up at the YMCA and to drive him the four blocks to the Federal Building in downtown Cincinnati. The YMCA had been a contributing factor to his weariness. Had he credited the FBI with enough imagination he would have blamed his stay at the Y upon a deliberate wish to depress him with the tattered cheeriness that filled the public rooms along with the grimy oak furniture and the countless unread Christian tracts.

The man took him to a new room in the Federal Building this time, a room like a dentist's office where a technician put hypodermics in him, measured his heartbeat and blood pressure, and even took X-ray photographs of his skull. These things were done, as someone explained, for "routine identification procedure." Bryce could not imagine what his heartbeat rate would have to do with identifying him; but he knew better than to ask. Then, abruptly, they finished, and the man who had brought him there told him that, as far as the FBI was concerned, he was free to go. Bryce looked at his watch. It was ten-thirty in the morning.

As he left the room and went down the corridor to the main entrance-way, he had another shock. Being led by a matron to the room he had just left, was Betty Jo. She smiled at him, but said nothing, and the matron hustled her past him and into the room.

He was astonished at his own reaction. Despite his weariness he felt a stomach-borne excitement, a kind of delight, at seeing her—even more so at seeing her frank-faced, chubby person in this absurd, ponderously severe corridor of the Federal Bureau of Investigation.

Outside the building he sat on the steps in the cold December sunlight and waited for her to come out. It was almost noon when she came and sat, heavily and shyly, beside him. With the cold air her perfume seemed warm—strong and sweet. A brisk young man with an attaché case came striding up the steps, and pretended not to see them sitting there. Bryce turned to Betty Jo and was surprised to see that her eyes were puffy, as though she had been recently crying. He glanced at her nervously. "Where've they been keeping you?"

"At the YWCA." She shuddered. "I didn't care for it much."

It was logical that they would have had her there, but he hadn't thought about it. "I've been at the other one," he said.

"At the YM. How did they treat you? The FBI, I mean." It seemed foolish to use all of those initials—YMCA, FBI.

"All right, I guess." She shook her head and then moistened her lips. Bryce liked the gesture; she had full lips, without lipstick, red now from the cold air. "But they sure asked a lot of questions. About Tommy."

Somehow the reference to Newton embarrassed him. He did not want to talk about the Anthean just then.

She seemed to sense his embarrassment—or shared it. After a pause she said, "Do you want to go eat lunch?"

"That's a good idea." He stood up and pulled his overcoat around him. Then he leaned down and helped her to her feet, taking both her hands in his.

By luck they found a good, quiet restaurant and they both ate a large lunch. It was all natural food, with no synthetics, and there was even real coffee to drink afterward, although it was thirty-five cents a cup. But they both had plenty of money.

They talked little during the meal, and they did not mention Newton. He asked her what her plans were and found that she had none. When they had finished eating he said, "What do we do now?"

She looked better now, more composed and cheerful. "Why don't we go to the zoo?" she said.

"Why not?" It seemed like a good idea. "We can take a taxi."

Possibly because it was the Christmas holiday season, there were very few people at the zoo, which suited Bryce perfectly. The animals were all indoors, and the two of them wandered from building to building, talking pleasantly. He liked the big, insolent cats, especially the panthers, and she liked the birds, the bright-colored ones. He was thankful and pleased that she cared for the monkeys no more than he did—he found them obscene little creatures—for it would have dismayed him had she, like so many women, found them cute and funny. He had never seen anything funny about monkeys.

He was also pleased to find that he could buy beer from a stand at, of all places, the entrance to the aquarium. They took their beers inside with them—although a sign told them plainly not to—and seated themselves in the dusky light before a large tank which contained an enormous catfish. The catfish was a fine, solid, placid-looking creature, with Mandarin mustaches and gray, pachydermous skin. It watched them dolefully while they drank their beer.

After they had sat in silence for a while, watching the catfish, Betty Jo said, "What do you think they'll do with Tommy?"

He realized that he had been waiting for her to bring up the subject. "I don't know," he said. "I don't think they'll hurt him or anything."

Betty Jo sipped from her cup. "They said he wasn't . . . wasn't an American."

"That's right."

"Do you know if he is, Doctor Bryce?"

He started to tell her to call him Nathan, but it didn't seem right to do that, just then. "I imagine they're right," he said, wondering how in the name of heaven they could deport him if they had found out.

"Do you think they'll keep him long?"

He remembered that X-ray of Newton's skeleton and the thoroughness of the FBI in testing him in the little dentist's office and abruptly he understood why they had tested him. They wanted to make sure that he was not an Anthean too. "Yes," he said. "I think they'll probably keep him for a long time. As long as they can."

She didn't reply and he looked over at her. She was holding her paper cup in her lap, with both hands, and staring down into it as if into a well. The flat, diffused light from the catfish's tank made no shadows on her face, and the unlined simplicity of her features and her poised, solid position on the bench made her appear like a fine and solid statue. He looked at her silently for what seemed a long time.

Then she looked over at him and it became obvious why she had been crying before. "You'll miss him, I suppose," he said. Then he finished his beer.

Her expression did not change. Her voice was soft. "I sure will miss him," she said. "Let's go look at the rest of the fish."

They looked at the rest of them, but there was none he liked so well as the old catfish.

When the time came to take a taxi back into town he realized that he had no address to give, that there was no particular place for him to go. He looked at Betty Jo, standing beside him now in the sunshine. "Where are you going to stay?" he asked.

"I don't know," she said. "I don't have any people around Cincinnati."

"You could go back to your family in . . . what was it?"

"In Irvine. It's not too far." She looked at him wistfully. "But I don't think I want to. We never got along."

He said, hardly thinking what it meant, "Do you want to stay with me? Maybe at a hotel? And then, if you wanted to, we could find an apartment."

She seemed stunned for a moment, and he was afraid he had insulted her. But then she took a step closer to him and said, "My God, yes. I think we ought to stay together, Doctor Bryce."

CHAPTER EIGHT

HE BEGAN DRINKING heavily again, during the second month of his confinement, and he was not altogether sure why. It was not loneliness, since now that he had confessed himself, as it were, to Bryce, he felt little wish for companionship. Nor did he feel that sense of intense strain he had labored with for years, now that the issues were simpler and the responsibilities almost nonexistent. He had only one major problem that might have served as an excuse for drinking: the problem of whether or not to continue with the plan, should he ever be permitted by the government to do so. Yet he did not often trouble himself with that—drunk or sober—since the possibility of his having any further choice in the matter seemed remote.

He still read a great deal, and had taken up a new interest in *avant-garde* literature, especially in the difficult, rigidly formal poetry of the little magazines—*sestinas, villanelles, ballades*, which, though somewhat weak on ideas and insight, were often linguistically fascinating. He even attempted a poem himself, an Italian sonnet in Alexandrines, but found himself alarmingly ungifted at it before he had struggled his way through the octave. He thought he might attempt it some time in Anthean.

He also read a good deal in the sciences and in history. His jailers were as liberal about supplying him with books as with gin; he never received so much as a raised eyebrow or a day's delay about anything he requested of the steward who was in charge of feeding him and cleaning his apartment. They seemed admirably skilled at serving him. Once, to see what would happen, he asked for the Arabic translation of *Gone With The Wind*, and the steward, unconcerned, had it for him in five hours. Since he could not read Arabic, and cared little for novels anyway, he used it as a bookend on one of his shelves; it was monumentally heavy.

The only serious objections he had to his confinement were that he sometimes missed being out of doors, and there were times that he would have liked to see Betty Jo, or Nathan Bryce, the only two people on the planet he could have claimed as friends. He had some feeling as well about Anthea—he had a wife on Anthea, and children—but the feeling was vague. He no longer thought very often about his home. He had gone native.

By the end of two months they seemed to have finished their physical tests, leaving him with a few unpleasant memories and a mild, recurring backache. Their interrogations by that time had become boringly repetitious; apparently they had run out of things to ask him. And yet no one had put to him the most obvious of questions: no one had asked him if he were from another planet. He was certain by that time that they suspected it, but it was never directly asked. Were they afraid of being laughed at, or was this a part of some elaborate psychological technique? At times he almost decided to tell them the entire truth, which they would probably disbelieve anyway. Or he could claim to be from Mars or Venus and insist on it until they were convinced he was a crackpot. But they could hardly be that foolish.

And then one afternoon they abruptly changed their technique with him. It came as a considerable surprise, and, finally, as a relief.

The questioning began in the usual fashion; his interrogator, a Mr. Bowen, had questioned him at least once a week from the beginning. Although none of the various officials had identified their positions to him, Bowen had always struck Newton as being a more important personage than the others. His secretary seemed a shade more efficient, his clothes a shade more expensive, the circles beneath his eyes a shade darker. Perhaps he was an under-secretary, or someone of consequence in the CIA. He was also obviously a man of considerable intelligence.

When he came in he greeted Newton cordially, seated himself in an armchair, and lit a cigarette. Newton did not like the smell of cigarettes, but he had long since given up protesting against them. Besides, the room was air-conditioned. The secretary seated himself at Newton's desk. Fortunately, the secretary did not smoke. Newton greeted them both affably enough; however, he did not offer to rise from the couch when they entered the room. There was, he recognized, a kind of petty cat-and-mouse game in all that; but he was not loath to play the game.

Bowen usually got to the point in a hurry. "I'll have to confess, Mr. Newton," he said, "that you have us as mystified as ever. We still don't know who you are or where you are from."

Newton looked straight at him. "I'm Thomas Jerome Newton, from Idle Creek, Kentucky. I'm a physical freak. You've seen my birth record in the Bassett County courthouse. I was born there in 1918."

"That would make you 70 years old. You look forty."

Newton shrugged his shoulders. "As I say, I'm a freak. A mutant. Possibly a new species. I don't think that's illegal, is it?" All of this had been said before; but he did not much mind saying it all again.

"It's not illegal. But we believe your birth record is forged. And that's illegal."

"Can you prove it?"

"Probably not. What you do you do pretty well, Mr. Newton. If you could invent Worldcolor films I imagine you could have a record forged easily enough. Naturally, a 1918 record would be a hard one to check on. Nobody still alive, and all. But there's still that matter of our not being able to locate any childhood acquaintances. And the even more odd matter that we can't find anyone who knew you prior to five years ago." Bowen stubbed out his cigarette, and then scratched his ear, as if his mind were somewhere else. "Would you tell me again why that is so, Mr. Newton?" Newton wondered idly if interrogators went to special schools to learn their techniques, like scratching the ear, or if they picked them up from the movies.

He gave the same answer he had given before. "Because I was such a freak, Mr. Bowen. My mother let hardly anyone see me. As you may have noticed I'm not the sort who chafes at confinement. Nor was confining a child very difficult to do in those days. Especially not in that part of Kentucky."

"You never went to school?"

"Never."

"Yet you're one of the best educated persons I've ever met." And then, before he could reply, "Yes, I know, you have a freak mind as well." Bowen stifled a yawn. He seemed thoroughly bored.

"That's right."

"And you hid out in some obscure Kentucky ivory tower until you were 65 years old, and nobody ever saw you or heard of you?" Bowen smiled wearily at him.

The conception of that was, of course, absurd, but there was nothing he could do about it. Obviously nobody but a fool would believe it, but he had to have a story of some kind or other. He could have taken more pains to create some documents and to bribe some officials to make a more convincing past for himself; but that had been decided against long before he'd left Anthea as being more risky than it would have been worth. Even getting an expert to forge the birth document had been a difficult and perilous business.

"That's right," he smiled. "Nobody ever heard of me, except a few long-dead relatives, until I was 65."

Abruptly Bowen said something that was new. "And then you decided to start selling rings, from town to town?" His voice had become harsh. "You had made for yourself—out of local materials, I suppose—about a hundred gold rings, all exactly alike. And you suddenly decided, at the age of 65, to start peddling them?"

That came as a surprise: they had not mentioned the rings before, although he had assumed that they must know about them. Newton smiled at the thought of the absurd explanation he was going to have to give for that one. "That's right," he said.

"And I suppose you dug up the gold in your back yard, and then made the gems with your Chem-Craft set, and did the engraving yourself with the point of a safety pin? All this so you could sell the rings for less than the gems alone were worth, to small jewelry stores."

Newton could not help being amused. "I'm an eccentric, too, Mr. Bowen."

"You're not that eccentric," Bowen said. "Nobody's that eccentric."

"Well, how would you explain it then?"

Bowen paused to light another cigarette. For all his show of irritation, his hand was perfectly steady. Then he said, "I think you brought the rings with you on a spaceship." He raised his eyebrows slightly. "How's that for a guess?"

Newton could not help being shocked, but he kept himself from showing it. "It's interesting," he said.

"Yes, it is. Even more interesting when you consider that we found the remains of a peculiar craft about five miles from the town where you sold your first ring. You may not know this, Mr. Newton, but that hull you left there was still radio-active in the right frequencies. It had been through the Van Allen belts."

"I don't know what you're talking about," Newton said. It was feeble, but there was nothing else for him to say. The FBI had turned out to be more thorough than he had expected. There was a lengthy pause. Then Newton said, "If I were an arrival by spaceship, wouldn't I have a better way of getting money than by selling rings?" Although he had thought for some time that he did not particularly care whether they found out the truth about him or not, Newton was surprised to find himself feeling ill at ease from these new questions, and from their directness.

"What would you do," Bowen said, "if you were from, say, Venus, and needed money?"

Newton found himself, for one of the first times in his life, having difficulty keeping his voice steady. "If Venusians could build spaceships, I suppose they could counterfeit money."

"And where would you find, on Venus, a ten-dollar bill to copy?"

Newton did not answer, and Bowen reached into his coat pocket, pulled out a small object, laid it on the table beside him. The secretary looked up momentarily, waiting for someone to say something, apparently so that he could write it down. Newton blinked. The thing on the table was an aspirin box.

"Counterfeit money brings us to something else, Mr. Newton."

He knew now what Bowen was going to talk about, and there was really nothing much he could do about it. "Wherever did you get that?" he said.

"One of our men ran across it while he was searching your hotel room in Louisville. That was two years ago—just after you broke your leg in the elevator."

"For how long have you been searching my rooms?"

"For a long time, Mr. Newton."

"Then you must have had reason to arrest me long before this. Why didn't you do it?"

"Well," Bowen said, "naturally we wanted to find out what you were up to first. With that ship you're making in Kentucky. And, you must be aware, the whole thing is pretty tricky. You've become a very rich man, Mr. Newton, and we can't go around arresting very rich men with impunity—especially if we are running what is supposed to be a sane government and our only charge against the rich man is that he's from some-place like Venus." He leaned forward, his voice softer. "*Is* it Venus, Mr. Newton?"

Newton smiled back. Actually the new information hadn't really changed things very much. "I never said it was anywhere but Idle Creek, Kentucky."

Bowen looked down at the aspirin box thoughtfully. He picked it up, weighed it in the palm of his hand. Then he said, "As I'm sure you already know, this box is made of platinum, which you'll admit is striking. It is also striking that, consid-ering the—the quality of the materials and workmanship, as the phrase goes, it is a very inept imitation of a Bayer Aspirin box. For example, it's a good fourth of an inch too large, and the colors are way off. Nor is the hinge made the way the Bayer people make them." He looked up at Newton. "Not that it's a better hinge—just different." He smiled again. "But probably the most striking thing about it is that there's no fine print on the box, Mr. Newton—just vague lines that look like print."

Newton was feeling uncomfortable, and angry with himself for not having remembered to destroy the box. "And what have you concluded from all that?" he said, knowing full well what they would have concluded.

"We concluded that someone had counterfeited the box as well as he could from a picture on a television commercial." He laughed briefly. "From television in an extreme fringe area."

"Idle Creek," Newton said, "is an extreme fringe area."

"So is Venus. And they sell Bayer Aspirin boxes, complete with aspirin, in the Idle Creek drugstore, for a dollar. There's no need at all to make your own, in Idle Creek."

"Not even if you happen to be a freakish eccentric, with very odd obsessions?"

Bowen still seemed amused—possibly with himself. "Not very likely," he said. "As a matter of fact I might as well end all of this fencing." He looked at Newton carefully. "One of the fascinating things about it is that a . . . a person of your intelligence could make so many blunders. Why do you suppose we happened to decide to pick you up when you were in Chicago? You've had two months to think about it."

"I don't know," Newton said.

"That's what I mean. Apparently you—Antheans, isn't it?— aren't altogether accustomed to thinking as we do. I believe any ordinary, human, detective magazine reader would have realized that we were bound to have had a microphone in your room in Chicago, when you were explaining yourself to Doctor Bryce."

He remained silent for a full minute, stunned. Then, finally, he said, "No, Mr. Bowen, apparently Antheans don't think as you people do. But then we wouldn't lock a person up for two months so that we could ask him questions, the answers to which we already knew."

Bowen shrugged his shoulders. "Modern governments move in mysterious ways, their wonders to perform. However, it wasn't my idea to arrest you; it was the FBI's. Somebody high up panicked. They were afraid you were going to blow the world up with that ferry boat of yours. In fact that has been their theory about you from the very beginning. Their operatives filed reports about the project and the assistant directors would try to decide when you were going to launch it against Washington or New York." He shook his head in mock sadness. "Ever since Edgar Hoover, that's been a damn apocalyptic outfit."

Newton got up abruptly and went to make himself a drink. Bowen asked him to fix three. Then he stood up himself and, hands in pockets, stared for a while at his shoes while Newton was making the drinks.

Handing the glasses to Bowen and the secretary—the secretary avoided his eyes as he took the drink—Newton thought of something. "But once the FBI heard your recording—I suppose you made a recording—they must have changed their minds about my purposes."

Bowen sipped his drink. "As a matter of fact, Mr. Newton, we've never let the FBI know about that recording. We merely gave them the order to make the arrest for us. The tape has never left my office."

That was another surprise. But surprises had been coming so rapidly that he was getting used to them. "How can you keep them from demanding the tape?"

"Well," Bowen said, "you might as well know that I have the good fortune to be director of the CIA. In a way, I outrank the FBI."

"Then you must be—what's his name, Van Brugh? I've heard of you."

"We're an elusive bunch in the CIA," Bowen—or Van Brugh—said. "Anyway, once we had the tape, we knew what we wanted to know about you. And we also determined from the fact of your confession, that if the FBI did pick you up—which as I told you they were on the verge of doing—you might well spill out the whole story to them. We didn't want that to happen, because we don't trust the FBI. These are perilous times, Mr. Newton; they might have solved the problem that we've been wrestling with by killing you."

"And you don't intend to kill me?"

"It's certainly occurred to us. I've never been for it mainly because—however dangerous you could be—doing away with you might be killing the goose that laid the golden eggs."

Newton finished his drink, then refilled the glass. "How do you mean that?" he said.

"Right now we already have, over at Defense, a good many projected weapons based on data we pilfered from your private file over three years ago. These are, as I say, perilous times; there are a lot of ways in which we could use you. I imagine you Antheans know a great deal about weapons."

Newton paused a minute, staring at his drink. Then he said, calmly, "If you heard me talking to Bryce you know what we Antheans did to ourselves with our weapons. I have no intention of trying to make the United States of America omnipotent. Nor, as a matter of fact, could I if I wished to. I'm not a scientist. I was picked for the trip because of my physical stamina, not my knowledge. I know very little about weapons—less than you do, I suspect."

"You must have seen, or heard about, weapons on Anthea."

Newton was regaining his composure now, possibly because of the drinks. He no longer felt defensive. "You've seen automobiles, Mr. Van Brugh. Could you explain, offhand, to an African savage how to make one? With only locally available materials?"

"No. But I could explain internal combustion to a savage. If I could find a savage in modern Africa. And, if he were a smart savage he might be able to do something with that."

"Probably kill himself," Newton said. "In any event, I do

not intend to tell you anything along that line, for whatever it might be worth to you." He finished another drink. "I suppose you could try torturing me."

"A waste of time, I'm afraid," Van Brugh said. "You see the reason we've been asking foolish questions of you for two months has been to conduct a kind of psycho-analysis. We've had cameras in here, recording eye-blink rates and things like that. We've already concluded that torture wouldn't work on you. You'd go insane too easily under pain; and we just can't learn enough about your psychology—guilt and anxieties and things like that—to do any kind of brainwashing on you. We've also loaded you with drugs—hypnotics, narcotics—and they don't work."

"Then what are you going to do? Shoot me?"

"No. I'm afraid we can't even do that. Not without the President's permission, and he won't give it." Then he smiled sadly. "You see, Mr. Newton, after all of the cosmic factors to be considered, the final one turns out to be a matter of practical, human politics."

"Politics?"

"It just happens that this is 1988. And 1988 is an election year. The President is already campaigning for a second term, and he has it on good authority—did you know that Watergate changed nothing—*nothing*—the President uses us, in the CIA, to spy on the other party?—that the Republicans are going to turn this whole business into something like the Dreyfus case if we don't either bring adequate charges against you or turn you loose with profuse apologies all around."

Abruptly, Newton laughed. "And if you shoot me, the President might lose the election?"

"The Republicans have your brother industrialists in the

NAM already worked up into a lather. And those gentlemen, as you probably know, wield a lot of influence. They also protect their own."

Newton was beginning to laugh even harder. It was the first time in his life that he had actually laughed aloud. He did not merely chuckle, or snicker, or snort; he laughed loudly and deeply. Finally, he said, "Then you'll have to let me go?"

Van Brugh smiled grimly. "Tomorrow. We're letting you go tomorrow."

CHAPTER NINE

FOR MORE THAN a year it had become increasingly difficult for him to know how he felt about many things. This was not a difficulty characteristic of his people, but he had acquired it somehow. During those fifteen years that he had learned to speak English, learned to fasten buttons, to tie a tie, learned batting averages, the brand names of automobiles, and countless other bits and pieces of information, so much of which had turned out to be unnecessary, during all that time he had never suffered from self-doubt, had never questioned that plan he had been chosen to carry out. And now, after five years of actually living with human beings, he was unable to tell how he felt about such a clear-cut matter as being released from prison. As for the plan itself, he did not know what to think, and as a consequence he hardly thought about it at all. He had become very human.

In the morning he was given his disguises again. It seemed

odd to put them on once more, before going back into the world, and it was silly as well, for from whom was he concealing himself now? Yet he was glad to have the contact lenses on again, the lenses that gave his eyes a more human appearance. Their light filters relieved his eyes from the strain of brightness that even the dark glasses he had been wearing continuously could not altogether protect him from. And when he put them on and looked in the mirror at himself, he was relieved to look human again.

A man he had not seen before took him from the room and down a hallway that was lighted by luminous panels—panels made under W. E. Corp. patents—and guarded by soldiers who carried guns. They entered an elevator.

The lights in the elevator were oppressively bright. He put on his dark glasses. "What have you told the newspapers about all this?" he asked, although he did not really care.

The man, though silent up to now, turned out to be quite affable. He was a short, stocky, bad-complexioned man. "That's not my department," he said pleasantly, "but I think they've said you were held in protective custody because of security reasons. Your work was vital to the national defense. Things like that."

"Will there be reporters waiting? When I get out?"

"I don't think so." The elevator stopped. The door opened into another guarded hallway. "We're going to sneak you out the back door, so to speak."

"Right away?"

"In about two hours. There are some routine things to do first. We have to process you out of this place. That's what I'm here for." They continued down the hallway, which was very long and, like the rest of the building, too brightly lighted. "Tell me," the man said, "what were you being held for anyway?"

"You don't know?"

"Those things are kept pretty quiet around here."

"Doesn't Mr. Van Brugh inform you of things like that?"

The man smiled. "Van Brugh doesn't tell anybody anything, except maybe the President, and he tells him only what he feels like telling."

At the end of the hallway—or tunnel, he was not certain which it was—was a door that led them into what appeared to be an oversized dentist's office. It was startlingly clean, with pale yellow tiles. There was a chair of the sort that dentists use, flanked by several uncomfortably new-looking machines. Two women and a man stood waiting, smiling politely, wearing pale yellow smocks that matched the tiles. He had expected to see Van Brugh—he wasn't certain why—but Van Brugh was not in the room. The man who had accompanied him here conducted him to the chair. He grinned. "I know it looks awful, but they won't do anything that hurts. Some routine tests, mostly for identification."

"My God," Newton said, "haven't you tested me enough?"

"Not us, Mr. Newton. I'm sorry if there's any duplication of what the CIA's been doing. But we're FBI, and we have to get this stuff for our files. You know, blood type, fingerprints, EEG, things like that."

"All right." He sat resignedly in the chair. Van Brugh had said that governments moved in mysterious ways, their wonders to perform. Anyway it shouldn't take too long.

For a while they prodded and inspected him with needles, photographic equipment and various metallic devices. They put clamps on his head to measure his brain waves, clamps on his wrists to measure his heartbeat. Some of their results he knew must be surprising to them, but they showed no surprise. It was all, as the FBI man had said, a matter of routine.

And then, after about an hour, they wheeled a machine up in front of him, putting it very close, and asked him to remove his glasses. The machine had two lenses, spaced like eyes, which seemed to regard him quizzically. There was a black rubber cup, like an eyecup, around each lens.

He was immediately frightened. If they did not know about the peculiarities of his eyes . . . "What are you going to do with that?"

The yellow-frocked technician took a small ruler from his shirt pocket and held it across the bridge of Newton's nose, measuring. His voice was flat. "We're just going to make some photographs of you," he said. "Won't hurt."

One of the women, smiling professionally, reached out for his dark glasses. "Here, sir, we'll just take these off now . . ."

He jerked his head away from her, putting up a hand to defend his face. "Just a minute. What kind of photographs?"

The man at the machine hesitated a moment. Then he glanced at the FBI man, now seated near the wall. The FBI man nodded affably. The man in the yellow smock said, "Actually, two kinds of pictures, sir, both at once. One's a routine I.D. photo of your retinas, to get the blood vessel pattern. Best identification you can make. Then the other picture is X-ray. We want the ridges at the inside of your occiput—the back of your skull."

Newton tried to get out of the chair. "No!" he said. "You don't know what you're doing."

Faster than he would have believed possible, the affable FBI man was behind him, pulling him back into the chair. He was unable to move. Probably the FBI man was not aware of it, but a woman could have held him easily. "I'm sorry, sir," the man behind him was saying, "but we have to have those pictures."

He tried to calm himself. "Haven't you been informed about me? Haven't you been told about my eyes? Certainly they know about my eyes."

"What about your eyes?" the man in the yellow gown said. He seemed impatient.

"They are sensitive to X-rays. That device . . ."

"Nobody's eyes can see X-rays." The man pursed his lips, obviously in irritation. "Nobody sees at those frequencies." He nodded to the woman and, smiling uncomfortably, she took his glasses off. The light in the room made him blink.

"I do," he said, squinting. "I see altogether differently from the way you do." Then, "Let me show you the way my eyes are made. If you'll release me I'll remove my . . . my contact lenses."

The FBI man did not release him. "Contact lenses?" the technician said. He leaned over closely, staring for a long moment into Newton's eyes. Then he drew back. "You're not wearing contact lenses."

He was feeling a sensation he had not felt for a long time— panic. The brightness of the room had become oppressive: it seemed to pulsate around him with the regularity of his heart-beat. His speech felt thick, drunken. "They're a . . . a new kind of lens. A membrane, not plastic. If you'll release me for a moment I'll show you."

The technician was still pursing his lips. "There's no such thing," he said. "I've had experience for twenty years with con-tact lenses and . . ."

Behind him the FBI man said something beautiful. "Let him try, Arthur," he said, abruptly releasing his arms. "After all, he's a taxpayer."

Newton let out a sigh. Then he said, "I'll need a mirror." He began fumbling in his pockets and, suddenly, panicked again. He did not have the special little tweezers with him, the ones designed for removing the membranes . . . "I'm sorry," he said, talking to none of them in particular. "I'm sorry, but I'll have to have an instrument. Maybe back in my room . . ."

The FBI man smiled patiently. "Now come on," he said. "We don't have all day. And I couldn't get in that room if I wanted to."

"All right," Newton said. "Then do you have a pair of small tweezers? Maybe I can do it with them."

The technician grimaced. "Just a minute." He mumbled something else, then went to a drawer. In a minute he had assembled a formidable set of shining instruments—tweezers, quasi-tweezers, and tweezer-like tools of unknown function. He laid them out on the table beside the dentist's chair.

One of the women had already handed Newton a circular mirror. He picked a blunt-ended small tweezer from the table. It was not very much like the one made for the job, but it might work. He clicked it experimentally a few times. Maybe a little too large, but it would have to do.

Then he found that he could not hold the mirror steady. He asked the woman who had given it to him to hold it. She stepped closer and took the mirror, holding it too near his face. He told her to back off a bit, then had to make her readjust its angle so that he could see properly. He was still squinting. The man in the yellow gown was beginning to tap his foot on the floor. The tapping seemed to keep time with the pulsation of the lights in the room.

When he brought his hand, carrying the tweezer, toward his eyes, the fingers began to tremble uncontrollably. He drew the hand back quickly. He tried again, but could not get the thing near his eye. His hand shook violently this time. "I'm sorry," he said, "Just a minute more ..." His hand drew back involuntarily from his eye, from fear of the instrument and of the damnably shaking, trembling, uncontrolled fingers. The tweezers fell from his hand, into his lap. He fumbled for them, then, sighing, looked at the FBI man, whose face was non-committal. He cleared his throat, still squinting. Why did the lights have to be so bright? "Do you suppose," he said, "that I could have a drink? Of gin?"

Abruptly the man laughed. But this time the laugh did not seem affable. It sounded sharp, cold, brutal. And it rang in the tiled room.

"Now come on," the man said, smiling indulgently, "Now come on."

Desperately now, he grasped the tweezers. If he could get only one of the membranes partly off, even if he damaged the eye, they could tell ... *Why didn't Van Brugh come and tell them?* It would be better for him to ruin one of his eyes than to submit them both to that machine, to those lenses that wanted to stare into his skull, to count, for some reason of idiots, the ridges on the back of his skull from the inside, counting them through his eyes, his sensitive eyes.

Abruptly, the FBI man's hands had clamped over his wrists again and his arms—those arms with so little strength in them when pitted against the strength of a human being—were

drawn once again behind his back and held. And then someone put a clamp around his head, tightening it at the temples.
"No!" he said, softly, trembling. "No!" He could not move his
head.

"I'm sorry," the technician said. "I'm sorry, but we have to
hold your head still for this." He did not sound at all sorry.
He pushed the machine directly up to Newton's face. Then he
turned a knob that brought the lenses and rubber cups up to
Newton's eyes, like binoculars.

And Newton, for the second time in two days, did something new to him, and very human. He screamed. He screamed
wordlessly at first and then he found himself forming words:
"Don't you know I'm not human? *I'm not a human being!*" The
cups had blocked off all light. He could see nothing, no one.
"I'm not a human being at all!"

"Now come on," the FBI man said, behind him.

And then there was a flash of silver light that was brighter,
to Newton, than the midday sun of deep summer is to a man
who has come from a dark room and has forced himself to
stare up at it, open-eyed, until his eyes had gone dark. Then he
felt the pressure leave his face, and knew that they had wheeled
the machine away.

It was only after he had fallen twice that they tested his eyes
and discovered that he was blind.

CHAPTER TEN

HE WAS KEPT incommunicado in a government hospital for six weeks, where the government doctors were able to do nothing whatever for him. The light-sensitive cells of his retinas had been almost completely seared: they were no more capable of visual distinctions than is a greatly over-exposed photographic plate. He could, after a few weeks, faintly make out light and dark, and could tell, when a large dark object was placed in front of him, that it was, indeed, a large, dark object. But that was all—no color was apparent, no form.

It was during this period that he began to think again of Anthea. At first his mind found itself recalling old and scattered memories, mostly of his childhood. He remembered a certain chess-like game that he had loved as a child—a game played with transparent cubes on a circular board—and he found himself recalling the complex rules whereby the pale green cubes took precedence over the gray ones when their configurations formed polygons. He remembered the musical instruments he had studied, the books he had read, especially the history books, and the automatic ending of his childhood at the age of thirty-two Anthean years—or forty-five, as the humans counted time—by marriage. He had not chosen his wife himself, although that was sometimes done, but had permitted his family to make the choice. The marriage had been an effective one, and pleasant enough. There had been no passion, but Antheans were not a passionate race. Now blind, in a United States hospital, he found himself thinking of his wife more fondly than he ever had before. He missed her, and wished she were with him. Sometimes he wept.

Not being able to watch television, he would listen at times to the radio. The government, he learned, had not been able to keep his blindness a secret. The Republicans were making considerable use of him in their campaign. What had happened to him they called an example of administrative high-handedness and irresponsibility.

After the first week he felt no rancor toward them. How could he be angry with children? Van Brugh offered embarrassed apologies: it had all been a mistake; he had not known the FBI hadn't been informed of Newton's peculiarities. He was aware that Van Brugh did not actually care, that he was only worried about what he, Newton, might eventually say to the press, what names he would name. Newton assured him, wearily, that he would say nothing except that it was all an unavoidable accident. No one's fault—an accident.

Then one day Van Brugh told him that he had destroyed the tape. He had known from the beginning, he said, that no one would believe it anyway. They would believe it to be a fake, or that Newton was insane, or anything except that it was true.

Newton asked him if he believed it was true.

"Of course I believe it," Van Brugh said quietly. "At least six people know about it and believe it. The President is one of them, and so is the Secretary of State. But we're destroying the records."

"Why?"

"Well," Van Brugh laughed coldly, "among other things we don't want to go down in history as the greatest assembly of crackpots ever to govern this country."

Newton set down the book with which he had been practicing Braille. "Then I can resume my work? In Kentucky?"

"Possibly. I don't know. We'll be watching you every minute for the rest of your life. But if the Republicans get in I'll be replaced. I don't know."

Newton picked up the book again. For a moment he had been interested, for the first time in weeks, in what was going on around him. But the interest had gone as quickly as it had come, leaving no trace. He laughed gently. "That's interesting," he said.

When he left the hospital, led by a nurse, there was a crowd waiting outside the building. In the bright sunlight he could see their silhouettes, and he could hear their voices. A passage in the crowd was kept open for him, probably by policemen, and the nurse led him through this to his car. He heard faint applause. Twice he stumbled, but did not fall. The nurse led him expertly; she would stay with him for months or years, as long as he needed her. Her name was Shirley, and as well as he could tell she was fat.

Suddenly his hand was taken and he felt it being gripped softly. A large person was in front of him. "Good to have you back, Mr. Newton." Farnsworth's voice.

"Thank you, Oliver." He felt very tired. "We have some business to discuss."

"Yes. You're on television, you know, Mr. Newton."

"Oh, I didn't know." He looked around, trying unsuccessfully to find the shape of a camera, "Where's the camera?"

"On your right," Farnsworth said, *sotto voce.*

"Turn me toward it please. Did someone want to ask me something?"

A voice, evidently that of a television commentator, spoke at his elbow. "Mr. Newton, I'm Duane Whitely of CBS television. Can you tell me how it feels to be out again?"

"No," Newton said. "Not yet."

The announcer did not seem taken aback. "What," he said, "are your plans for the future? After the experience you've just been through?"

Newton had finally been able to pick out the camera, and he faced it now, almost totally unconscious of his human audience, both here in Washington and behind sets all over the country. He was thinking of another audience. He smiled faintly. At the Anthean scientists? At his wife? "I was, as you know," he said, "working toward a space exploration project. My company was engaged in a rather large undertaking, to send a craft out into the solar system, to measure the radiations that have so far made interplanetary travel impossible." He paused for breath, and realized that his head and shoulders were aching. Perhaps it was the gravity again, after so long a time in bed. "During my confinement—which was in no way unpleasant—I have had a chance to think."

"Yes?" the announcer said, filling the pause.

"Yes." He smiled gently, meaningfully, even happily toward the camera, toward his home. "I've decided that the project was over-ambitious. I am going to abandon it."

1990: ICARUS DROWNING

CHAPTER ONE

NATHAN BRYCE HAD first discovered Thomas Jerome Newton through a roll of caps. He rediscovered him through a phonograph record. He found the record as accidentally as he had found the caps, but what it meant—at least in part—was much more immediately evident than the meaning of the caps had been. This happened in October of 1990, in a Walgreen drugstore in Louisville, a few blocks from the apartment where Bryce and Betty Jo Mosher lived together. It was seven months after the time of Newton's tiny farewell address on television.

Both Bryce and Betty Jo had saved the larger part of their World Enterprises salaries, and it was not really necessary that Bryce work for a living, at least not for a year or two. He had, however, taken a job as consultant to a manufacturer of scientific toys—a job which he felt, with a certain satisfaction, brought his career in chemistry full circle. He was on his way home from work one afternoon when he stopped in the drugstore. His purpose was to buy a pair of shoe-laces, but he paused at the doorway when he saw a large metal basket of phonograph records beneath a sign that read, Closeout 89c. Bryce had always been a bargain-hunter. He thumbed through a few of the record tags, toyed for a moment with one or two, and then encountered an amateurishly turned-out one that, by its title, immediately startled him. Since the time that phonograph records had become small steel balls, the manufacturers ordinarily packed them in little plastic boxes fastened to a large plastic tag. The tag displayed the arty picture and the usually ridiculous commentary that the old-fashioned quadraphonic albums had carried. But the tag on this one was merely of cardboard, and there was no picture. In an inexpensive attempt at the required artiness, the record's title made use of the trite device of lower case printing throughout. It read: *poems from outer space.* And, on the reverse side of the card: *we guarantee you won't know the language, but you'll wish you did! seven out-of-this-world poems by a man we call "the visitor."*

Without any hesitation at all Bryce took the record to the trial booth, put the ball in its channel, and turned on the switch. The language that came out was weird indeed—sad, liquid, long-voweled, rising and falling strangely in pitch, completely unintelligible. But the voice, without question, was that of T. J. Newton.

He turned the switch off. At the bottom of the record card was printed: *recorded by "the third renaissance," twenty-three sullivan street, new york . . .*

The "third renaissance" was in a loft. Its office staff consisted solely of one person, a dapper young Negro with an enormous mustache. This person was, fortunately, in an expansive mood when Bryce dropped into his office, and he readily explained that "the visitor" of the record was a rich nut named Tom something-or-other who lived someplace-or-other in the Village. This nut, it seemed, had approached the recording outfit himself and had underwritten the cost of making and distributing the record. He might be found at a coffee-and-booze house around the corner, a place called The Key and Chain . . .

The Key and Chain was a relic of the old coffee-houses that had gone out in the seventies. Along with a few others it had managed to survive by installing a bar and selling cheap liquor. There were no bongo drums and no announcements of poetry readings—their era had passed away a long time before—but there were amateurish paintings on the walls, cheap wooden tables placed at random around the room, and what few customers there were studiously dressed like bums. Thomas Jerome Newton was not among them.

Bryce ordered himself a whisky and soda at the bar and drank it slowly, resolved to wait for at least several hours. But he had only begun his second drink when Newton came in. At first Bryce did not recognize him. Newton was slightly stooped and he walked more heavily than before. He had on his usual dark glasses, but now he carried a white cane, and he was wearing, of all absurdities, a gray fedora hat. A fat uniformed nurse led him by the arm. She took him to an isolated table in the back of the room, seated him, and left. Newton faced toward the bar and said, "Good afternoon, Mr. Elbert." And the bartender said, "I'll be right with you, dad." Then the bartender opened a bottle of Gordon's gin, put it on a tray with a bottle of Angostura bitters and a glass, and carried the tray over to Newton's table. Newton produced a bill from his shirt pocket, handed it to him, smiled vaguely, and said, "Keep the change."

Bryce watched him intently from the bar while he groped for the glass, found it, and poured himself a half tumbler full of gin, and added to this a generous dash of bitters. He used no ice and did not stir the drink but began sipping it immediately. Abruptly Bryce began to wonder, almost in panic, what he was going to say to Newton, now that he'd found him. Could he rush over from the bar, clutching his whisky-and-soda, and say, "I've changed my mind in the past year. I want the Antheans to take over, after all. I've been reading the newspapers, and now I want the Antheans to take over." It all seemed so ridiculous now that he was actually with the Anthean again—and Newton seemed, now, like such a pathetic creature. That shocking conversation in Chicago seemed to have taken place in a dream, or on another planet.

He stared at the Anthean for what seemed a long time, remembering the last time he had seen the Project, Newton's ferry boat, beneath the Air Force plane that had carried him, together with Betty Jo and fifty others, from the site in Kentucky.

For a moment, thinking about this, he almost forgot where he was. He remembered that fine big absurd ship they had all been building down in Kentucky, remembered the pleasure he had taken in his work on it, the way he had, for a time, been so absorbed in solving those problems of metals and ceramics, of temperature and pressure, that he had felt his life was actually involved in something important, something worth-while. Probably by now parts of the ship were beginning to rust—if the FBI hadn't already sealed the whole thing in thermoplastic and sent it off to be filed in the basement of the Pentagon. But whatever had happened, it certainly would not have been the first means of possible salvation to get the official treatment.

Then, in the mood that this line of thinking had put him in, he thought *what the hell*, stood up, walked over to Newton's table, sat down and said, his voice calm and deliberate, "Hello, Mr. Newton."

Newton's voice seemed equally calm. "Nathan Bryce?"

"Yes."

"Well," Newton finished the drink in his hand. "I'm glad you came. I thought that maybe you would come."

For some reason the tone of Newton's voice, possibly the casual unconcern in it, rattled Bryce. He found himself suddenly feeling awkward. "I found your record," he said. "The poems."

Newton smiled dimly. "Yes? How did you like them?"

"Not very much." He had been trying for boldness in saying that, but felt as though he only managed to be pettish. He cleared his throat. "Why did you make it, anyway?"

Newton remained smiling. "It's amazing how people don't think things out," he said. "At least that's what a man with the CIA told me." He began pouring himself another drink of gin, and Bryce noticed that his hand trembled while he did it. He set the bottle down shakily. "The record is not of Anthean poems at all. It's something like a letter."

"A letter to whom?"

"To my wife, Mr. Bryce. And to some of the wise people at my home who trained me for . . . for this life. I've hoped it might be played on FM radio sometime. You know, only FM goes between planets. But as far as I know it hasn't been played."

"What does it say?"

"Oh, 'Good-bye.' 'Go to hell.' Things of that sort."

Bryce was feeling increasingly uncomfortable. For a moment he wished he had brought Betty Jo with him. Betty Jo would be marvelous for restoring sanity, for making things understandable, even bearable. But then Betty Jo happened to believe that she was in love with T. J. Newton, and that might even be more awkward than this. He remained silent, not knowing what in the world to say.

"Well, Nathan—I suppose you won't mind if I call you Nathan. Now that you've found me, what do you want of me?" He smiled beneath the glasses and the ridiculous hat. His smile seemed as old as the moon; it was hardly a human smile at all.

Bryce suddenly felt embarrassed, at the smile, at Newton's grave, tired, terribly weary tone of voice. He poured himself a drink before answering, inadvertently clinking the bottle mouth against the glass. Then he drank, looking hard at Newton, at the flat, unreflecting green of Newton's glasses. He held the clear plastic drinking glass between both hands, elbows on the table, and said, "I want you to save the world, Mr. Newton."

Newton's smile did not change, and his reply was immediate. "Is it worth saving, Nathan?"

He had not come here to exchange ironies. "Yes," he said. "I think it's worth saving. I want to live out my life, anyway."

Abruptly Newton leaned forward in his chair toward the bar. "Mr. Elbert," he called, "Mr. Elbert."

The bartender, a small man with a sad, pinched face, looked up from his reveries. "Yeah, dad?" he said gently.

"Mr. Elbert," Newton said, "are you aware that I'm not a human being? Did you know that I'm from another planet, Anthea by name, and that I came here on a spaceship?"

The bartender shrugged. "I've heard that," he said.

"Well I am and I did," Newton said. "Oh, I did indeed." He paused, and Bryce stared at him—shocked not by what Newton had said, but by a childish, adolescent, silly quality in his voice. What had they done to him? Had they only blinded him?

Newton called to the bartender again. "Mr. Elbert, do you know why I came to this world?"

This time the bartender did not even look up. "No, dad," he said, "I haven't heard."

"Well, I came to save you." Newton's voice was precise, ironical, but there was a hint of hysteria in it. "I came to save you all."

Bryce could see the bartender smile a private smile. Then, still behind the bar, he said, "You'd better get with it, dad. We need saving fast."

Then Newton hung his head, whether in shame, despair or fatigue Bryce could not tell. "Oh, yes indeed," he said in what was almost a whisper. "We need saving fast." Then he looked up and smiled at Bryce. "Do you see Betty Jo?" he asked.

That caught him off guard. "Yes . . ."

"How is she? How is Betty Jo?"

"She's all right. She misses you." And then, "As Mr. Elbert said, 'We need saving fast.' Can you do it?"

"No. I'm sorry."

"Isn't there a chance?"

"No. Of course not. The government knows all about me . . ."

"You told them?"

"I might have; but it wasn't necessary. They seem to have known for a long time. I think we were naïve."

"Who? You and I?"

"You. I. My people back home, my wise people ..." He called out softly, "We were naïve, Mr. Elbert."

Elbert's reply was as soft. "That a fact, dad?" He sounded genuinely concerned, as if he really believed, for a moment, what Newton was talking about.

"You came a long way."

"Oh, I did indeed. And on a small ship. Sail on, sail on, and on ... It was a very long trip, Nathan, but I spent much of the time reading."

"Yes. But I didn't mean that. I meant you've come a long way since you've been here. The money, the new ship ..."

"Oh I've made a lot of money. I still make a lot. More than ever. I have money in Louisville and money in New York and five hundred dollars in my pocket and a medicare pension from the government. I'm a citizen now, Nathan. They made me a citizen. And perhaps I could draw unemployment insurance. Oh, World Enterprises is a going concern, without my running it at all, Nathan. World Enterprises."

Bryce, appalled by the strange way that Newton looked and talked, found it difficult to keep his eyes on him, so he looked down at the table instead. "Can't you finish the ship?"

"Do you think they'd let me?"

"With all your money ..."

"Do you think I want to?"

Bryce glanced up at him. "Well, do you?"

"No." Then, suddenly, Newton's face fell into its older, more composed, more human appearance. "Or yes, I suppose I do want to, Nathan. But not enough. Not enough."

"Then what about your own people? What about your family?"

Newton smiled that unearthly smile again. "I imagine they'll all die. But, then, they'll probably outlive you."

Bryce was surprised at his own words. "Did they ruin your mind when they ruined your eyes, Mr. Newton?"

Newton's expression did not alter. "You don't know anything at all about my mind, Nathan. That's because you're a human being."

"You've changed, Mr. Newton."

Newton laughed softly. "Into what, Nathan? Have I changed into something new, or back into something old?"

Bryce did not know what to say to this, and he kept silent.

Newton poured himself a small drink and set it on the table. Then he said, "This world is doomed as certainly as Sodom, and I can do nothing whatever about it." He hesitated. "Yes, a part of my mind is ruined."

Bryce, searching for protest, said, "The ship . . ."

"The ship is useless. It had to be finished on time, and now there isn't enough time. Our planets won't be close enough to one another for seven more years. They are already moving apart. And the United States would never let me build it. If I built it they would never let me launch it. And if I did launch it they would arrest the Antheans who returned on it, and probably blind them. And ruin their minds . . ."

Bryce finished his drink. "You said you had a weapon."

"Yes, I said that. I was lying. I don't have any weapon."

"Why should you lie . . . ?"

Newton leaned forward, putting his elbows carefully on the table. "Nathan. Nathan. I was afraid of you then. I am afraid now. I have been afraid of all manner of things every moment I have spent on this planet, on this monstrous, beautiful, terrifying planet with all its strange creatures and its abundant water, and all of its human people. I am afraid now. I will be afraid to die here."

He paused, and then when Bryce still said nothing, began to talk again. "Nathan, think of living with the monkeys for six years. Or think of living with the insects, of living with the shiny, busy, mindless ants."

Bryce's mind, for several minutes, had been becoming extremely clear. "I think you're lying, Mr. Newton. We aren't insects to you. Maybe we were at first, but we aren't now."

"Oh yes, I love you, certainly. Some of you. But you're insects anyway. However, I may be more like you than I am like me." He smiled his old, wry smile. "After all, you're my field of research, you humans. I've studied you all my life."

Abruptly the bartender called to them, "You fellows want clean glasses?"

Newton drained his. "By all means," he said, "bring us two clean glasses, Mr. Elbert."

While Mr. Elbert was sopping the table with a large orange rag Newton said, "Mr. Elbert, I've decided not to try to save us, after all."

"That's too bad," Elbert said. He set the clean glasses on the damp table. "I'm sorry to hear that."

"It is a pity, isn't it?" He groped for the newly placed gin bottle, found it, poured. Pouring gin, he said, "Do you see Betty Jo often, Nathan?"

"Yes. Betty Jo and I live together now."

Newton took a sip from his drink. "As lovers?"

Bryce laughed softly. "Yes, as lovers, Mr. Newton."

Newton's face had become impassive, with the impassivity that Bryce had learned was a mask for his feelings. "Then life goes on."

"Well, what in the name of heaven do you expect?" Bryce said. "Of course life goes on."

Suddenly Newton began to laugh. Bryce was astonished: he had never heard him laugh before. Then, still trembling with the fag end of laughter, Newton said, "It's a good thing. She won't be lonely now. Where is she?"

"At home in Louisville, with her cats. Drunk probably."

Newton's voice was steady again. "Do you love her?"

"You're trying to be stupid," Bryce said. He had not liked the laughter. "She's a good woman. I'm happy with her."

Newton smiled now, gently. "Don't misunderstand my laughing, Nathan. I think it's a fine thing, the two of you. Are you married?"

"No. I've thought about it."

"By all means marry her. Marry her and go off on a honeymoon. Do you need money?"

"That's not why I haven't married her. But I could use some money, yes. Do you want to give me some?"

Newton laughed again. He seemed greatly pleased. "By all means, yes. How much do you want?"

Bryce took a drink. "A million dollars."

"I'll write you a check." Newton groped in his shirt pocket, pulled out a check book, set it on the table. It was from the Chase Manhattan Bank. "I used to watch that show about the million dollar check on television," he said. "Back home." He pushed the check toward Bryce. "You fill it out and I'll sign it."

Bryce took his Woolworth ballpoint pen from his pocket and wrote his name on the check and then the figures $1,000,000. Then he wrote out, carefully, One Million Dollars. He pushed the book across the table. "It's made out," he said.

"You'll have to direct my hand."

So Bryce stood up, walked around the table, placed the pen in Newton's hand and held it while the Anthean wrote out, Thomas Jerome Newton, in a clear, steady hand.

Bryce put the check in his billfold. "Do you remember," Newton said, "a motion picture, shown on television, called *A Letter to Three Wives?*"

"No."

"Well I learned to write English long-hand from a photograph of that letter, twenty years ago on Anthea. We had clear reception, from several channels, of that motion picture."

"You have good clear handwriting."

Newton smiled. "Of course I have. We did everything extremely well. Nothing was overlooked, and I worked very hard to become an imitation human being." He turned his face up toward Bryce's, as if he could actually see him. "And of course I succeeded."

Bryce, saying nothing, returned to his seat. He felt that he should show sympathy, or something, but he felt nothing at all. So he remained quiet.

"Where will you and Betty Jo go? With the money?"

"I don't know. Maybe to the Pacific, to Tahiti. We'll probably take an air-conditioner with us."

Newton was beginning to smile the moon smile, the unearthly Anthean smile, again. "And stay drunk, Nathan?"

Bryce was uneasy. "We might try that," he said. He did not really know what he was going to do with a million dollars. People were supposed to ask themselves what they would do if someone gave them a million dollars, but he never had asked himself that. Maybe they would, indeed, go to Tahiti and stay drunk in a hut, if there were any huts in Tahiti any more. If not, they could stay at the Tahiti Hilton.

"Well I wish you Godspeed," Newton said. And then, "I'm glad I could do something with the money. I have an awful lot of money."

Bryce stood up to leave, feeling tired and a little drunk. "And there's no chance . . . ?"

Newton smiled up at him even more strangely than before; the mouth beneath the glasses and hat was like an awkwardly curved line in a child's drawing of a smile. "Of course, Nathan," he said. "Of course there's a chance."

"Well," Bryce said. "I thank you for the money."

Because of the dark glasses Bryce could not see Newton's eyes, but it seemed to him as though Newton were looking everywhere. "Easy come, easy go, Nathan," he said. "Easy come, easy go." Newton began to tremble. His angular body began to lean forward and the felt hat fell silently on to the table, showing his chalk-white hair. Then his Anthean head fell on to his spindly Anthean arms and Bryce saw that he was crying.

For a moment Bryce stood quiet, staring at him. Then he walked around the table and, kneeling, laid his arm across Newton's back and held him gently, feeling the light body trembling in his hands like the body of a delicate, fluttering, anguished bird.

The bartender had come over and when Bryce looked up the bartender said, "I'm afraid that fellow needs help."

"Yes," Bryce said. "Yes, I guess he does."

THE HUSTLER

To the strangers he plays in darkened pool halls, at first "Fast" Eddie Felson seems like a sloppy pool player with bright eyes and an extraordinary grin. It's not until real money is on the line that they find out Eddie is a hustler of the first order. But Eddie's got ambitions and wants to quit his two-bit hustling for the big time. And when he sets his sights on Minnesota Fats, the best pool player in the country, he knows this match will be a true test of his skill—and he knows he can win. But what Eddie doesn't know is that the game of pool isn't all about skill. It's about guts, stamina, and, above all, character.

Fiction

THE COLOR OF MONEY

Twenty years have passed since "Fast" Eddie Felson conquered the underground pool circuit. During that time he married and opened his own pool hall. But he's left that all behind and is now badly in need of money, and pool is all he knows. On the beautiful aquamarine waters of the Florida Keys, he ropes his former rival Minnesota Fats into a series of exhibition matches in the hopes of picking up a cable TV deal. But playing the old master, a terrible feeling nags at him—that he's sat on his talent and the best part of him is now gone. And when he vows to get back in the game—seriously this time—he finds a challenging road ahead, and the only thing standing in his way is himself.

Fiction

The year is 2063. Earth's energy resources are dangerously close to being depleted, a new world superpower has upset America's global dominance, and the threat of another ice age looms large. Fortunately, there is one man brave enough—and perhaps foolish enough—to venture beyond the planet to find the mineral resources that will secure the country's future: Ben Belson. One of the richest men in the world, Belson is haunted by personal demons and wanted for his unlawful space travel, but he will stop at nothing to fulfill his crucial mission—and discover a future greater than he could ever have imagined.

Fiction

ALSO AVAILABLE

Mockingbird
The Queen's Gambit

VINTAGE BOOKS
Available wherever books are sold.
www.vintagebooks.com